"...y Would You Settle For This ...d Of Relationship When You Could Have Something Real?"

"This feels real to me," he said, walking into the bedroom.

He sat down on the edge of her bed and then snagged her wrist, drawing her close. "Doesn't this feel real to you?"

She swallowed hard. She wasn't explaining this the right way. She wanted him to say that there was more between them than an arrangement, but there was no way that was going to happen tonight.

"I guess so."

He pulled her even closer, wrapped his arms around her waist and rested his head on her shoulder. The move was unexpected and she didn't know what it meant. But she realized that analyzing Dominic's actions wasn't going to bring her the answers she sought. Not tonight.

Dear Reader,

I hope you have enjoyed the previous two books in MORETTI'S LEGACY. The last book is one of my favorite themes…a boss/secretary story with a twist. Dominic Moretti has been trying to track down the person who has sold his company's secrets. Imagine his shock and outrage when the path leads straight back to his office and to his secretary, Angelina De Luca.

I really enjoyed writing these stories because of the chance it afforded me to explore my own Italian-American heritage and of course the wonderful city of Milan.

Dominic was the least likely of the Moretti brothers to believe and trust in love. Moretti Motors's success was easy for him to rely on because he knew he had the skills to make the company profitable. But he has never seen himself as lovable. Sexy, yes.

Angelina does see Dominic's potential as a mate, but battling against his own instincts to convince him that they can have happily ever after is hard.

Happy reading!

Katherine Garbera

KATHERINE
GARBERA

THE MORETTI ARRANGEMENT

Published by Silhouette Books
America's Publisher of Contemporary Romance

ISBN-13: 978-0-373-76943-8
ISBN-10: 0-373-76943-1

THE MORETTI ARRANGEMENT

This edition published by arrangement with Harlequin Books S.A.

Visit Silhouette Books at www.eHarlequin.com

Printed in U.S.A.

Books by Katherine Garbera

Silhouette Desire

The Bachelor Next Door #1104
Miranda's Outlaw #1169
Her Baby's Father #1289
Overnight Cinderella #1348
Baby at His Door #1367
Some Kind of Incredible #1395
The Tycoon's Temptation #1414
The Tycoon's Lady #1464
Cinderella's Convenient Husband #1466
Tycoon for Auction #1504
Cinderella's Millionaire #1520
††*In Bed with Beauty* #1535
††*Cinderella's Christmas Affair* #1546
††*Let It Ride* #1558
Sin City Wedding #1567
††*Mistress Minded* #1587
††*Rock Me All Night* #1672
†*His Wedding-Night Wager* #1708
†*Her High-Stakes Affair* #1714
†*Their Million-Dollar Night* #1720
The Once-A-Mistress Wife #1749
****Make-Believe Mistress* #1798
****Six-Month Mistress* #1802
****High-Society Mistress* #1808
**The Greek Tycoon's Secret Heir* #1845
**The Wealthy Frenchman's Proposition* #1851
**The Spanish Aristocrat's Woman* #1858
Baby Business #1888
§*The Moretti Heir* #1927
§*The Moretti Seduction* #1935
§*The Moretti Arrangement* #1943

††King of Hearts
†What Happens in Vegas…
**The Mistresses
*Sons of Privilege
§Moretti's Legacy

KATHERINE GARBERA

is a strong believer in happily-ever-after. She's writen more than thirty-five books and has been nominated for *Romantic Times BOOKreviews'* Career Achievement awards in Series Fantasy and Series Adventure. Her books have appeared on the Waldenbooks/Borders bestseller list for series romance and on the *USA TODAY* extended bestsellers list. Visit Katherine on the Web at www.katherinegarbera.com.

To Rob, for showing me that
there really is such a thing as having it all.

One

"Sìgnore Moretti, is everything okay?" his secretary, Angelina De Luca, asked as he returned to his office.

Dominic didn't know what he'd do without her. She was even more of a godsend now that they had a leak in the Moretti organization.

"No, Angelina, I'm not okay. I need to see Antonio in my office immediately."

"*Sì,* Signore Moretti."

"Angelina?"

"Sì?"

"I've given you leave to call me Dominic."

"Yes, you have, but when you come into the office looking as angry as you do today…I think it's best that I observe all rules of propriety and lie low."

"Have I ever treated you unfairly?" Dominic asked.

"Not at all," Angelina said with a smile.

Dominic smiled back at her. He'd be interested in his pretty secretary, if it weren't for his family's curse.

A curse that promised that each generation of Morettis would be either lucky in love or lucky in business, but never in both.

Lorenzo Moretti, Dominic's grandfather, had been very lucky in business but had died a bitter old man. Dominic's father Giovanni had been and still was very lucky in love. He and Dominic's mother shared a love that was deep and abiding.

And now his brothers were screwing things up for their generation despite the blood vow they'd all taken in their teens. They had promised each other they would be the generation of Morettis to take back the proud name that had once been revered on both the Grand Prix track and in the world of luxury sports cars.

He lived in Milan but traveled the world entertaining guests at Team Moretti's VIP rooms at all of the Formula 1 Grand Prix races. As the CEO of Moretti Motors he was currently overseeing the launch of a revamped model of their 1970s classic Vallerio Roadster.

The car had been named for one of the fastest F1 drivers ever. Lorenzo Moretti's best friend, Pierre-Henri Vallerio.

"Is there anything I can do?" Angelina asked.

"Just keep doing your job," Dominic said. He'd been relying more and more on his assistant to make sure that things were running smoothly. Last year he had realized someone was stealing Moretti secrets. It had started with partial engine design and modifications showing up in cars made by their chief competitor, ESP Motors. Before long, Dominic, Antonio and Marco had realized that the spy was someone working for their organization.

They had traced the leak back to the corporate offices here in Milan. But they had been unable to uncover anything further.

Marco was busy as Team Moretti's F1 driver. He didn't have the time to delve into what was happening in the corporate offices of Moretti Motors.

Antonio was busy dealing with the Vallerio family. He had to continuously ensure that the use of the Vallerio name on the new Moretti Motors Vallerio Roadster was well within the rights of the contract Pierre-Henri had signed years ago.

So that had left Dominic with the task of making sure the spy was caught. And he would take great pride in prosecuting the thief. He desperately wanted retribution.

"I'll get Antonio down here as soon as possible," his secretary said. "Also you had a call from Ian Stark. I put him through to your voice mail."

"Thank you, Angelina."

Dominic left his assistant's desk and entered his office, which had been occupied by every CEO of Moretti Motors since his grandfather had purchased this building in 1964. No expense had been spared when Lorenzo had designed this office. He said that he wanted everyone who entered this room to know that the man who sat at the desk was one of power.

A man who could make things happen, Dominic thought. He walked over to the wall where his *nono*'s portrait hung. In it, Lorenzo stood next to his first F1 car—the first Moretti Motors car that he had designed and driven in the Grand Prix.

He looked up at his grandfather and was reminded of the promises he, Antonio and Marco had made to each other. He was so aware that their dream of rebuilding Moretti Motors had in his brothers' eyes been accomplished. But Dominic wanted more.

He wanted the legacy his grandfather had left to them to continue. He wanted Moretti Motors to become synonymous with luxury, speed and greatness. And he couldn't do that while someone was selling the secrets they'd spent the last three years developing.

Angelina called Antonio and greeted him politely when he came down to see Dominic. Once the two men were in Dominic's office, the smile faded from her face. She loved her job at Moretti Motors—not that she thought she'd have it for much longer.

She was in a bad place. It didn't help that she'd allowed herself to be manipulated. At the end of the day she was responsible for her actions.

And she knew that any kind of explanation she came up with as to why she'd done what she had…well, that wasn't going to get her any sympathy from Dominic Moretti.

She was half in love with the man. Really, what wasn't to love? He was tall, muscular…a fine-looking man with an earthy sexiness.

He had dark eyes that seemed to stare into the very heart of her. But she knew he had no mystical powers—he couldn't really see the lies she kept carefully hidden away.

"Angelina?" Dominic's voice came from the intercom.

"Sì?"

"Please make a reservation for myself and my parents for Friday at Cracco-Peck."

"Will nine be a good time?"

"Sì," Dominic said.

She made the reservation and then sent an e-mail to Dominic and his parents with the confirmation information. She was privy to every detail of Dominic's life…well, just the business ones, but Dominic Moretti was a man who lived for his company. He wasn't just the CEO of Moretti Motors, he *was* Moretti Motors. His brothers also shared responsibility for the company, but it was Dominic who lived and breathed it.

And she was slowly stealing the secrets that he

had worked so hard to develop. In fact, just two days ago she'd gone to London to meet with Barty Eastburn of ESP Motors to give him the company's latest plans.

Her mobile phone rang and she glanced at the caller ID. Her brother. "Renaldo, I can't talk now."

"We have to, Ange. I need something else. Eastburn isn't satisfied with what you've given him."

"Renni, I really can't. Everyone here is being watched. I—"

"They are going to kill me, Ange. I know it's not fair to ask you to save me again, but I have no one else."

She wanted to cry. Her brother was the only family she had and yet she'd never been able to rely on Renni. He was younger than she was by a mere fifteen months, but she felt years older.

"I'll see what I can do. What does he want?"

"You'll have to come to London. He's booked a ticket in your name."

Angelina didn't know if she could keep doing this. She didn't want her brother to die and she knew he wasn't being melodramatic. He'd gambled and lost big time to exactly the kind of men that she had warned him to avoid. And now it seemed the only way to pay off his debts was for her to keep betraying her boss.

"I'll…I can't decide right now," she said. "I don't like doing this, Renni."

There was silence on the line, but in the background she heard the noises of the dock. How had her brother gotten so lost?

"I understand, Ange. You've done more than a sister should have to."

She heard that note in his voice. The one that always scared her because it signaled that Renni was about to do something really stupid and dangerous. And as much as she wanted him to take responsibility for his life, she didn't want to have to visit her brother in the hospital again.

"I'll be there," she found herself saying.

"Thanks, Ange."

"This has to be the last time, Renni. If I do this you come back to Milan with me. No more gambling."

"I'll do it. All of it. I promise."

She hung up the phone and rubbed her temples, knowing better than to believe Renni's promises. She knew that he meant the words that at this moment Renni wanted to stop. But wanting and doing were two different things.

The door to Dominic's office opened and he and Antonio came out. The men were still talking and for a moment she wanted to just say that she quit and run away.

But instead she eavesdropped on their conversation and heard Antonio mention that they had finished the design of the Vallerio Roadster and that the new engine design was on his desk.

"Angelina, can I see you in my office?" Dominic asked after Antonio had departed.

"Yes. Do I need to bring a notepad?"

"No."

She stood and preceded Dominic into his office. Once there she went to a guest chair and sat down. He closed the door and just stared at her for a long minute and she realized that the ruse was up.

Somehow Dominic must have discovered she had been stealing secrets for ESP Motors' Barty Eastburn. And as sad as she was to be losing her freedom, she also felt relief. She wasn't cut out for the kind of subterfuge she'd had to engage in over the past year.

"I've asked you in here because I need your help setting a trap."

She actually felt the blood drain from her face. Oh, God, what was she going to do? "A trap?"

"I had two sets of plans made for the new engine configuration. I want you to send one to Emmanuel and one to Stephan."

"Wouldn't it be better to just bring both men in and question them?" she asked. She didn't want Dominic to suspect either of the two company executives. They were good men with families, she thought.

Dominic shook his head. "I've hired an outside investigations firm and they have advised me that the spy has to be caught red-handed. Otherwise there's something called plausible deniability and I'm not about to let the man who stole from me get away with it."

Angelina nodded. She felt a sense of doom as she realized that this really was the end for her. There was no way that Dominic's firm wasn't going to figure out that she was the leak.

The following afternoon found Dominic satisfied that he'd set everything in motion that he possibly could to catch the spy. He'd hired Ian Stark of Stark Security. He and Ian had gone to college together. After graduation they'd both gone into their families' businesses.

Stark Security had been in the business of protecting the rich and famous for over a hundred years, not as a bodyguard service but as an intellectual properties security firm. Ian protected the secrets of the famous. And he did a damn fine job of it.

Now he was going to catch Dominic's corporate spy. In fact he was already en route now. Which was cause for celebration, Dom thought.

However, his brothers were all occupied right, and though he was having dinner later this evening with his parents, he wanted to celebrate now.

Or was he just looking for an excuse to ask his lovely secretary out for a drink?

Yes, he was.

He walked out of his office and found her desk empty. He was just sitting down in her chair to write her a note when she came back in.

"Ah, there you are," he said.

"Yes, here I am. Did you need something?"

"Yes. Get your coat, we are going out for a drink to celebrate."

She smiled at him. That shy sweet smile that had played a part in a number of fantasies for him lately.

"What are we celebrating?"

"Success," he said.

"I'll drink to that," she said.

He stood and realized how small his assistant was and how very feminine. The dress she wore today was cut close to her body and had a plunging neckline. The skirt flounced around her legs as she stepped closer to him.

Her curly hair reached almost to her jaw, and swung around her creamy skin whenever she moved her head. She had stepped close to get to her desk, but he didn't move away.

He took a good look at her kissable lips. How the lower lip was fuller than the top one. He started leaning down toward her before he realized what he was doing.

"Dominic?"

"Hmm?"

"What are you thinking about?" she asked. She seemed nervous and licked her lower lip as she watched him.

God, he wanted her mouth under his. He wanted to know exactly what she tasted like, what she felt like in his arms. And now that he was taking care of the problems at Moretti Motors, he could move his focus elsewhere.

An affair was exactly what he needed, and

Angelina was the woman he wanted. "I'm thinking about you."

"In what way?" she asked.

She seemed almost nervous. Normally he preferred a more sophisticated woman—a woman who knew the score and didn't become attached. And in the last two years working with Angelina he knew she wasn't that type of girl.

Maybe he should walk away, but he couldn't. He'd tried to ignore Angelina since she'd started working for him. At first it had been relatively easy since they'd still been struggling to bring the company back up to speed, but for the last year or so he'd started seeing Angelina more and more as an attractive woman and not just his secretary.

"I'm thinking about kissing you," he told her.

Her hand covered her lips. "Why?"

"Why shouldn't I?" he asked.

"We work together, Dom," she said.

"Is that a problem?"

She tipped her head to the side, one inky curl felling across her face, and he tucked it back behind her ear before she could. Her skin was soft, but then he'd expected it to be. He *hadn't* expected her to turn her head to the side and rub her cheek against his finger for a brief moment.

"I think it is a problem," she said. "I like my job too much to compromise it."

He dropped his hand and stepped away from her. He could respect that. "You are a top-rate assistant and you would be hard to replace."

"So you'd fire me?" she asked.

"No. Just transfer you to another department. I wouldn't want you to feel pressured to date me…it's just that lately I can't seem to stop thinking of you in terms that aren't exactly suited to the office."

"I've had a few thoughts about you, too," she said.

He arched one eyebrow at her. "Have you? Want to tell me what those thoughts were?"

She shook her head. "I don't think that's a good idea. But I will join you for the celebratory drink. What are you celebrating?"

"Stark Security found our leak. As of tomorrow morning that person will be in police custody and we will be back on track."

She flushed. "Did they give you the name?"

"No, not yet. Ian doesn't like to deliver that type of news over the phone."

"How did he figure it out?"

"I'll tell you while we are having our drink."

She glanced down at her calendar. "Oh, I can't go. I forgot it was Wednesday."

"What do you have on Wednesdays?" he asked.

"I meet my book club. This week I'm hosting, so I can't be late. I'm sorry, Dominic. But congratulations to you on finding the leak."

She gathered her purse and coat and walked out the door. Dominic rested his hip against the edge of her desk and watched her leave. He had a feeling of what might have been but let it go. Having Angelina at his side was important to the future success of Moretti Motors.

Two

Angelina didn't think twice about the call she was going to make. She couldn't do it anymore—work for Dominic and continue to sell his secrets to ESP Motors. She was still worried about her brother. Renaldo's safety had been her only motivator.

But it had gone on long enough. Tonight she'd had to put her own happiness on hold to take care of her younger brother…stop it, she thought. There was no excuse she could give even to herself that would justify what she'd done.

Instead of going home when she'd left the offices, she'd wandered through the streets of

Milan, ending up at the Piazza del Duomo. Now she sat at a small café nursing a glass of wine and watching the evening crowds.

Their lives seemed so simple, so uncomplicated compared to hers. How had her life gotten so messed up? How long before her freedom was taken from her and she ended up in prison?

She knew Dominic was going to prosecute her. And she couldn't blame him. *Dios,* she wished she'd made a different choice when Renaldo had first come to her.

But after she'd said no and the men he'd owed the money to had beat him…well, visiting her brother in the hospital and seeing him so close to death had changed her mind.

No matter that she'd been half in love with Dominic Moretti, Renaldo was her brother and she couldn't allow him to be killed when she had the means to save him.

Somehow she doubted that explanation was going to make any difference to Dominic.

"Angelina?"

She glanced up to see Marta Kingsley, another secretary from Moretti Motors, standing by her table. "*Ciao,* Marta."

"Can I join you?"

"Of course. Are you alone?"

"I'm meeting a guy that I met online," Marta said.

"Online dating? I can't believe you do that."

"It's a lot of fun actually. And I don't think I'm going to meet Mr. Right this way but hey, I'm an American in Milan and it gets me out of my apartment."

Angelina laughed for the first time since she realized that Dominic had found his corporate spy. "It does get you out."

Marta smiled. She was very pretty and her life seemed uncomplicated. Angelina knew that Marta went out at least three times a week.

"You should try it."

"I don't think so," Angelina said. "My life is pretty complicated right now."

"I get that. Dominic is one demanding boss."

"Yes, he is." And he was also a very enchanting man. Her mind kept replaying his asking her out for a drink. God, she'd wanted to say yes. But she'd known if Dominic found out she was his spy, he'd be doubly angry that she'd led him on.

"Do you like working for him? The one time I filled in for you, I was scared the entire time of doing something wrong."

"He's not that bad. He seems gruff, but he's not really. And if you do your job to the best of your ability…well, that's all he asks."

"I'm just glad that he's not my boss," Marta said. She stared at a man standing on the corner, looking about. "Ah, I think that's my date."

"Which one?"

"The one in the cranberry-colored T-shirt. Um…he looks different than his online profile photo."

"Don't they all?" Angelina asked. "I tried online dating for a while, but never found a man who matched what he said in his profile."

"That's true enough, but then I don't exactly match my profile, either."

"You lied about yourself?" Angelina asked.

"Just fudged a few details. Like I found that being an American drew the wrong sort of men, so I dropped my nationality off the page and I said I was twentysomething instead of thirty."

"Oh, why? Do you want to start a relationship with lies between you?" Angelina asked.

"Not really, but I think everyone lies about something."

Angelina wanted to argue, but found she couldn't. Thanks to her own actions she'd become one of the people she used to loathe. "I guess you're right."

"Don't sound so disappointed," Marta said. "The world we live in is one based on half-truths." Her mobile rang and she glanced at the caller ID. "That's my date. He must not recognize me. I'll see you at work tomorrow."

"*Ciao,* Marta."

Her friend left and Angelina felt a sense of…melancholy. She was sad that she'd let Renaldo change her. But then she'd always known he would. From the day their parents had died in a car crash when she was eighteen, she'd known her life would change.

Renaldo had been sixteen, an age at which some men, men like Dominic would have been mature enough to handle responsibility, but Renni wasn't cut from the same cloth as Dominic Moretti.

Heck, not many were, she thought. She swallowed the last of her wine. She had to stop thinking of Dominic as some sort of romantic leading man. He wasn't. No matter that he'd asked her out for a drink tonight. No matter that he'd almost kissed her.

He wasn't for her. He'd never been the man for

her. Even if she hadn't sold his secrets to save her brother, Dominic was never going to be her man. He was out of her league.

She got to her feet deciding it was time to head home. She wondered what tomorrow would bring. Would the police be waiting at the office and arrest her?

Marta caught her eye as she walked past the open-air patio and waved at her. Angelina waved back, trying to pretend she was like the others in the Piazza. But deep inside she knew she would never be like everyone else again.

Dominic had a nice evening with his brothers and parents, then returned home to wait for Ian to drop by.

Looking about his empty house, he realized there was something missing from his workaholic life. He could never settle down to love one woman, would never leave himself open to that kind of betrayal again. But he could see himself in a long-term affair.

The doorbell rang and Dom went to answer it. He greeted his friend, then groaned as he glanced at the car parked in front of his house. "A Porsche?"

"I like the car. It's the first one I bought with my own money," he responded.

"Still, they are a major competitor of mine. Show some respect."

"Ah, Dom, you know that I have two Moretti Motors cars in my garage at home."

"You couldn't drive one here?"

"Nope. It'll drive Tony nuts to see that Porsche outside," Ian said with a quick grin.

Dom thought of what his brother's reaction would be and smiled at his friend. "Yes, it will. So, what do you have for me?" he asked as they seated themselves in the living room.

"I think I should wait for your brothers to get here."

"Marco can't make it."

"Racing business?" Ian asked.

"No, his new wife."

"I thought you guys were cursed. No marriages for any of you."

"Marco's wife, Virginia, is the granddaughter of the woman who cursed *Nono*. She thinks her marriage to Marco broke the curse."

"Could it be that simple?" Ian asked.

Dominic had no idea; he shrugged. "They seem happy."

"I guess that's all that matters when it comes to relationships."

"Happiness?" Dominic asked.

"That's been my experience," Ian said. "If a woman is happy, then everything is good."

Dominic had no such experience; his affairs were usually brief. He'd always believed if a relationship was structured like a business deal he'd have a better chance at making it work.

"Dom, you've got a big piece of trash in front of your house," Antonio said as he came through the door.

"Most people don't consider a Porsche trash, Tony."

"I can't speak to others' ignorance," Antonio said.

Ian laughed and stood to shake his hand. "Good to see you."

"You as well. So, did you find our leak?" Antonio asked.

"I did. I think it's going to shock you both."

Dom had seen it all in his time as CEO of Moretti Motors. They'd encountered corporate spying before and had implemented internal security measures but it looked as though their prior loss-prevention techniques had failed. "Nothing would shock me."

Ian looked straight at Dom. “Not even the fact that the leak is your secretary, Angelina De Luca?”

“What? Are you sure?” Dom asked. He crossed to the bar on one wall, poured two fingers of whiskey into a highball glass and swallowed in one long draw. Filled with rage, he wanted to smash something. He couldn’t believe that he’d entertained the thought of starting an affair with her while she had been betraying him. He’d relied on her….

“Positive. She’s been feeding information to ESP Motors. I saw the last drop myself.”

“How the hell is that possible?” Dom asked.

Antonio spoke up. “She’s had free rein of our corporate offices. She knows everything.”

“I know that,” Dom said.

“What do you want to do next?” Ian asked. “I have enough evidence to go to the police and press charges. We can have her arrested.”

“Do you have enough to prove ESP was behind it? Did you catch them in the act?”

ESP was the company founded by Nigel Eastburn, Lorenzo Moretti’s biggest rival on and off the racetrack. Both men had started their own car companies after retiring. The launch of the

Vallerio model had pushed Lorenzo ahead of Nigel. In the 1980s, when Moretti Motors had started to fail, ESP Motors—named after Nigel and his two partners, Geoffrey Saxby and Emmitt Pearson—had moved ahead. That was why Moretti Motors wanted their new Vallerio Roadster to be a success—to take back the pride that they'd lost when ESP had become the name synonymous with roadsters.

"I'm sure I can get irrefutable proof that ESP is behind the espionage if you give me another week or so. I need to make sure the person contacting Angelina isn't working independently," Ian said.

"Who is it?" Dominic asked.

"Barty Eastburn."

"Nigel's grandson? That is big. Well, I'd rather take him down than just Angelina." Dominic hoped he appeared nonchalant, that the rage he felt toward his secretary was well hidden.

"Angelina can't get off without punishment," Antonio said.

"She won't," Dom said. The fierceness of his tone seemed to startle Antonio.

"Don't do anything rash, Dom," his brother said.

"*I* will handle it. Ian, please let me know as soon as you are ready to spring the trap on Barty."

"Do you think Angelina will help us with it?" Ian asked.

"Yes, she will."

"How can you be certain?" Ian asked.

"Because I'm not going to give her a choice."

Ian and Antonio left shortly after ten and Dominic paced broodingly through his home. He had dialed Angelina's mobile number several times but hung up before the call connected. He was so angry right now that he knew talking to her was the wrong thing to do.

But as he paced around his home office he knew he couldn't wait until morning to confront her. He needed a plan of action. He needed something to occupy his mind.

He stopped under the portrait of his *nono,* Lorenzo Moretti. The man who had the vision to make Moretti Motors what it was today. And Dominic shook his head.

His brothers and he had tried very hard to make sure that *Nono*'s problems weren't theirs.

But being cursed with women…well, that was something that Dom seemed to share with his grandfather. Angelina's betrayal cut deeper than he'd expected.

He walked to the bar and poured himself another drink. He tipped his head back and drained the glass. What was he going to do about Angelina?

He realized that he held all the cards. He could do whatever he wanted with Angelina. And he wanted *her.* He wanted her completely.

But what he really wanted, he realized, was to make her *pay.*

Revenge wasn't a noble trait, but she had stolen from him. All the while he'd been attracted to her and so trusting of her, and she'd been plotting with his enemy. The question was why?

He couldn't stand to be alone with his thoughts anymore. He put his glass down, looked up Angelina's address on his BlackBerry and called a cab. He'd had too much to drink to drive safely.

He had the cab take him to Angelina's apartment building. She lived in a decent place and there was nothing about her lifestyle that indicated she needed more money. Certainly not the kind of money she'd earn by selling him out.

What did she need the money for?

He paid the driver and walked toward her

building. It was chilly on this spring evening but not cold. He stood on the street looking up at the windows for a minute. He had no plan and that was odd for him. He was acting on an impulse and he had no idea how it would play out.

But he didn't turn around. He went into her building. There was no doorman and he went to the elevator and pushed the button for her floor, pleased Ian had supplied him with so much of Angelina's personal information.

The apartment building was less attractive from the inside than it had been from the street. The floors were dirty and showed signs of age. The building itself smelled faintly of onions and dust.

Was this it? Was living in this dismal place what had motivated her to try to get some extra cash?

He shook his head. He wasn't going to sympathize with Angelina. She'd taken from him and she'd have to pay.

He rapped on her door. It was so late, he wondered if she'd even answer. He heard no sounds from inside her apartment and knocked again. This time he heard footsteps.

"Who is it?"

"Dominic."

He heard the snick of the lock being disengaged and then the door opened inward. She leaned forward and glanced up and down the hall. "Are you alone?"

"*Sì.* May I come inside?"

She stepped back and let him in. Pivoting on her heel, she walked into her apartment. Dominic followed close on her heels right into the living room.

"Do you want to sit down?" she asked.

After he'd taken a seat in a large leather arm chair his anger got the better of him. He couldn't stop himself from blurting out, "Why?"

Angelina didn't appear the least surprised that she'd been found out.

"It's complicated," she told him. "I'm not sure that I can explain it."

"You're a smart woman. Try."

She took a deep breath and he thought he saw sadness in her eyes, but he refused to feel sympathy for her.

"I have a brother—"

"What does he have to do with you stealing from me?" Dominic asked.

"Everything," she said. "He's the reason why I got involved with ESP Motors."

"Does he work for them?" Dominic asked, pushing to his feet.

"Not exactly. He's a bit of a gambler," Angelina said. She wrapped her arms around her waist. "Renni doesn't have a sense of responsibility like you do."

"What do you mean by that?"

"My brother is a weak man. He gambles, a lot. And when he gets into trouble he comes to me for help. He's my little brother, so I do what I can."

"Because your parents are gone?"

"Yes, we only have each other."

"What kind of trouble is he in?"

"He gambles in illegal places because he really doesn't have the funds for high-stakes poker in casinos."

"So he owes criminals money?"

She nodded. "Yes. But this time I couldn't cover his debts and he met a man in a London pub who offered him money in exchange for Moretti Motors' secrets."

"A man who works for ESP?" Dominic asked.

"He not only works for ESP, he's an executive there. Renni got really drunk and ended up talking about me to this man."

"Who is this man?"

"Barty Eastburn. Renni told him I was your assistant and Barty offered to help him out if I gave him information from your office."

Dominic was torn by her revelations. He tried to tell himself he was motivated by the fact that she could give him Barty Eastburn to prosecute, but he knew deep inside that he wanted Angelina and this was a way to have her.

"I'm going to make you an offer, Angelina. And it is not negotiable. If you accept it I will keep you and your brother out of jail. If you do not, then you will be arrested tomorrow morning." He wanted Angelina and knew he couldn't let her go to prison. His desires in this moment were torn between Moretti Motors and a woman. Perhaps he had his grandfather's curse. Dominic refused to make Lorenzo's mistakes, though. Angelina wouldn't be his downfall the way the women in Lorenzo's life had been his.

By the look on her face he knew he had her exactly where he wanted her.

Three

Angelina had no idea what Dominic would offer her in exchange for staying out of jail, but she'd take it. Anything would be better than incarceration. *Anything.*

She hated the thought that she had no options, but she realized she'd given away her choices when she'd allowed Renni to manipulate her. She'd always believe that if she was going to make a stupid decision, then she couldn't complain about the consequences.

"What do you have in mind?" she asked. Her voice sounded wispy to her own ears. Obviously she wasn't going to do a good job at hiding her nervousness.

Dominic stood and walked over to where she sat on the couch. Sitting down next to her, he touched her face with one finger as he had earlier today in the office. His touch was warm, exciting all of her nerve endings.

"I'm so glad you know the truth," she said, the words coming out without her intention.

"Are you?" he asked, stroking her face.

She shivered with awareness her fear of jail time melting away under his touch. In fact, she thought of nothing but Dominic and how he felt next to her. "Yes. I hated lying and sneaking around. It was horrible."

Dominic stared at her. "Then why did you do it?"

"He's my brother, Dominic. I had to help him if I could," she said. "Wouldn't you do the same thing for Antonio or Marco?"

"You know I would. But I can't just forgive this, Angelina."

"I know. Moretti Motors is your life."

"That doesn't mean I'm an automaton."

"No, you're not," she said, turning her head into his touch. He cupped her cheek, his fingers tunneling into her hair. She opened her eyes and looked up at him. Attraction sprang to life between them.

She kissed his hand while watching his eyes. Saying no to him earlier had been hard. Harder than she'd thought it would be, but she shouldn't have been surprised. She'd been attracted to Dominic from the first moment she'd met him.

"What do you have in mind?" she asked.

"Something very intimate."

That made her pulse race. She shouldn't be excited by his deep voice, but she was. "Like what?"

"Like an agreement between you and me."

She felt a twinge of nervousness but quickly quelled it. This was Dominic. Being in his bed was a much better alternative than being in prison. "I'm listening."

"I want you to become my mistress, Angelina."

Hearing the words out loud was surprising though she'd known he was attracted to her. "Um…I'm not sure I'd really like that."

"You'd prefer prison?"

"Of course not. Are there any other options?"

"No. You gave them up when you started stealing from me."

"What choice did I have? They were going to kill my brother!"

Dominic looked at her. "Am I such a monster that you couldn't come to me?"

"No," she said. There was no way she was going to tell Dominic Moretti that her pride had kept her from opening up about Renni and his problems. She couldn't stand the thought of the man who needed no one knowing that she couldn't handle her own problems. One of the things he said he liked about her was her independence.

"Then what was it?"

She stood and walked around her very common little living space. There were two things she valued in the room: a picture of her parents in front of the Trevi Fountain on their honeymoon and a vase that her brother had painted for her when she'd left for college. The vase was silly and clearly amateurish, but he'd made it for her and it meant the world to her.

"You aren't going to be able to understand," she said, realizing that a man who lived in a house like Dominic's wasn't going to get why she'd sell secrets to save her brother. To a man who had more money than Midas, even if it was only recently, he wouldn't get that sometimes if you were poor circumstances were out of her control.

He walked over to her, making the room seem smaller by his sheer physical presence. "That doesn't really matter. We can't go into the past and change it. We can only move forward."

"There is one thing we can change. I am supposed to make another drop at the end of the week."

"What information?"

"I don't know. Um…Barty is going to call me tomorrow to confirm the details."

"Haven't you paid off your brother's debts yet?"

More times than Dominic would appreciate hearing about. But as long as Renni stayed in London he was tempted into heavy play and she ended up bailing him out again. She knew she needed to be firmer with him, but hadn't been able to. "No, not yet."

He took her jaw in his hand, surprising her with his quick move. "Don't lie to me anymore."

He wasn't hurting her at all, but the firmness of his grip kept her in place. "What do you want to hear?"

"The truth would be nice," he said.

If only it were that simple. She had always wondered if she'd taken the action she had because she'd wanted to get Dominic's attention. Had her desire to have him see her as more than just an ultraefficient secretary led to this?

He loosened his grip on her jaw, slid his hand down her neck to her shoulder. "Tell me what's going on, Angelina."

She swallowed hard. "I've paid off his original debt, but Barty keeps getting him into games that he can't handle and when he loses…I have to get more information so Barty will keep paying off Renni's debts."

"So now you are stuck between me and your loyalty to your brother."

"I don't see that at all. I'm stuck between you and jail."

"Either way you have a choice to make."

"Yes, I do," she said, quietly. "Why are you offering me this deal?"

Dominic didn't say anything for a long minute. She felt the seconds ticking by slowly as she waited.

"Because I want you," he said. "And I always get what I want."

"Why do you want *me?*"

"You're an attractive woman," he said.

"Damned by faint praise."

He liked her attitude and the fact that she wasn't behaving like a victim. It was that spunkiness that had long drawn him to her in the first place.

"There's a spark between us," he added.

She tipped her head to the side. "Yes, there is."

"I want you as my mistress for six months."

"And at the end of that time will I still have a job?"

"If I feel I can trust you," Dominic said.

"That's fair enough. You're being more than generous," she said. "Um…what does your mistress do?"

"She denies me nothing. I will make love to you wherever I desire. You will live in an apartment that I have for you."

"Why?"

He shrugged. Telling her that keeping a separate apartment would make the ending of their relationship easier wasn't going to go over well. He knew that from experience.

But he didn't want to use either of their homes—that would make the relationship seem paramount.

"Dominic?"

"I like having a residence that will just be for our affair. And, your place is not in a convenient location."

"So if I accept this…"

"Arrangement," he supplied.

"Arrangement, then. If I accept it, you will not press charges against me or my brother?"

"Has your brother passed on information to ESP himself?"

"No, he hasn't. Other than getting money from Barty, I don't think he has any specific knowledge of what's gone on."

Dominic didn't like her brother at all. The other man was taking terrible advantage of Angelina and she was letting him. A part of him knew it was that same trait in her that was going to allow her to accept his offer.

"Very well, but your brother must return to Milan. And if he has any further dealings with Eastburn, his immunity will be revoked."

Angelina bit down hard on her lower lip. "I don't know if he can do that, Dominic. He will promise you anything, but in the end he always breaks his word."

"That won't be your concern."

"How do you figure?"

"You have bailed him out enough. It's time to let him stand on his own."

Dominic knew he wouldn't back down on this point. Angelina's days of selling her soul for her brother were over.

"If I don't agree to this?"

"Then the both of you will be prosecuted and sent to jail."

"I guess I always knew you would find me out and my whole life would change."

Dominic looked around her apartment. It was small and cozy and from the arrangement of the furniture and the prints on the wall he could tell she'd done her best to make this place her home. "You are right. Your life is about to change. You can let it happen around you or you can take control."

"How do you figure?"

"Well, now you can stop lying. And stop keeping all your fears bottled inside you."

"What's in this for you?" she asked. "I know I'm not an unattractive woman, but I'm hardly the type of woman who inspires these kinds of gestures in men."

Dominic thought about her question. "I can't

speak to their actions, but you are the woman I want. It's turned into an obsession, Angelina. And I know that I don't want to let you have that kind of control over me."

She frowned at him. "That sounded like a compliment at first, but then not so much. Are you saying I'm some kind of devil you are trying to exorcise?"

He laughed and for the first time since he'd heard her name from Ian he felt an end to the relentless emotion of anger that had been blanketing him. "My attraction to you is powerful, but I don't want to exorcise you from my life."

"You don't?"

"No, Angelina. I don't. I want to take you to my bed and let the attraction between us run its course. I wanted you before I found out you were selling my secrets," he said. "That hasn't changed. Making you my mistress will give us both a chance to enjoy the physical attraction between us."

"What if what we have turns out to be nothing but a spark and it dies out quickly?"

"Do you honestly think it will?" he asked, pulling her into his arms and kissing her.

Having Dominic's arms around her was both everything she'd ever wanted and everything she'd feared. She didn't have the experience to handle a man like Dominic yet at the same time this felt right.

The intensity in his eyes awakened something deep inside her that she'd always been afraid of. She knew she was weak-willed, witness the current idiocy with her brother, but there was something ephemeral about Dominic. He touched parts of her that she'd always ignored. Parts that she didn't want to have to acknowledge.

She was over her head, but then that was nothing new and for once she wanted to just let go of her fears and worries. And in Dominic's arms she could do so.

His lips rubbed over hers, making her stop thinking and just experience him. His tongue teased her lips but didn't enter her mouth and his hands moved over her neck and shoulders, up to her face.

She liked the feel of his hands against her face. He made her feel cherished and beautiful. Two things she could safely say she'd never experienced before. But that didn't mean she knew how to handle it or him. Or that she even wanted to.

"I think that answers the question of attraction," he said, ending their kiss.

She blinked up at him, realizing how silly it had been to think that the attraction between them wasn't real.

"You're staring at my mouth."

"It's so perfectly formed," she said. "It looks hard but your lips were soft against mine."

"Were they?"

He quirked one eyebrow at her, stroking his finger down the side of her neck. She shivered as he rubbed the pad of his finger over her pulse. She felt it increase and fought to keep her expression serene. To somehow keep him from guessing that he had any affect on her. But she knew that he was used to being around much more sophisticated women.

"Yes," she said. "You're a very attractive man."

"Thanks," he said.

Startled, she had to laugh. "You are too much."

There was an innate charm that imbued everything he did. She wondered if it stemmed from his childhood. Or maybe his birth order. Something about being the oldest Moretti and knowing that he'd take the lead in anything he and his brothers did had made him very aggressive.

He was watching her carefully and she felt as if he were seeing all the way to her soul.

She shrugged and tried to pull away from him.

But he slid his fingers around the back of her neck and held her still.

"Don't. I won't allow you to back down from me, Angelina. Your passion is mine."

"Is it?"

He nodded. He was so sure of himself. So confident that she wanted to just let him take control of this situation. More than he already had. She wanted to make love to him and then fall asleep in his arms, but that was dangerous thinking. Dominic was the one man she knew who could really dominate her life.

"I don't know if I can do this," she said at last. "I want to, but giving myself to you, Dominic, is scary."

"Scary? Why?"

"I'm excited and nervous and turned on all at once. That's a very heady mix of emotions."

"You're a heady woman, Angelina."

"Am I?"

"Yes, every curve of your body entrances me and makes me want to caress you. I have to hold you in my arms, feel you pressed against me."

The fear she felt abated at his words. She knew that if she let herself go to him and became his mistress she'd never be the same.

Enough, she thought. She couldn't keep dilly-dallying in her mind. She knew what she had to say to him. What she had to do.

She wanted an affair with him and she wanted to make up for the skullduggery of the last several months. She wanted a chance to get to know Dominic Moretti.

He cupped the back of her head and drew her closer to him. She leaned forward and found herself within an inch of him.

Her lips suddenly felt dry and she licked them. He touched his tongue to her lips, following the trail of her tongue. He tasted good, like scotch and a taste that she knew was uniquely Dominic.

The worries she'd carried for so long faded to the back of her mind. "Okay."

"Okay?"

"I'll be your mistress."

"Six months. For six months you will be mine completely and then we will move on."

"Agreed," she said.

He brushed his lips over hers, angled his head and thrust his tongue deep into her mouth, claiming her and she knew she'd never be the same again.

He tunneled his fingers into her hair and held

her head back while he plundered her mouth. She slipped her arms up around his neck, moving up on her tiptoes so she could be closer to him.

His hands slid down her shoulders to her back. She felt his hands skimming over her spine and then they came to rest at her hips. He lifted her off her feet and into his arms as he turned and sat down on the sofa.

Her legs fell on either side of his hips and she found herself straddling him. She lifted her head and looked down into his midnight eyes.

She saw passion in the lines of his Roman features. His hands as they moved over her incited further desire in her. And for the first time in her life she realized she was doing something that was just for her. She wasn't motivated by anything other than the desire to be with Dominic.

Four

Dominic forgot about revenge and corporate espionage when he took Angelina in his arms. He twisted his hands in her thick short hair and held her head as he plundered her mouth. He needed to make sure she knew that she was his. As of this moment she belonged to him.

He didn't analyze the intelligence of his actions, the way he usually did. Angelina De Luca wasn't like other women, and that had never been more clear to him than right now.

Her lips were full and soft under his. Her tongue met his with small darts and she held on to him with surprising strength. She moaned deep in her throat as he slid his hands up her hips to her waist.

The pants she wore frustrated him because he couldn't easily touch her skin. "From now on you will wear only skirts."

"I will?"

"Yes. As my mistress…you will be mine, Angelina. You will do what I ask, when I ask it."

"I'm not really the type of woman—"

He put his fingers over her lips. "Forget who you were before this moment, Angelina. From now on you are mine."

"Forever?"

"For the next six months."

That should give him enough time to have his fill of her body. Should. But would it? He only knew that this moment was one that he'd waited for and he wasn't about to let Angelina De Luca mean more to him than an other mistress would.

"Okay," she said. Putting her hands on either side of his face. "Six months. What else?"

"Later," he said, pulling her head back to his. "Tomorrow morning I'll have my lawyer draw up the agreement."

She started to pull back, but he held her close.

Bringing his mouth to hers, he pushed her doubts aside with the force of his will.

He drew his hands over her body, enjoying the feel of her. He'd worked late with her many nights, wishing they were spending the hours in a much different way. Now she was here in his arms.

He slipped his hands between their bodies and lifted up the hem of her blouse. The skin at her waist was smooth and cool to his touch. She shifted back on his thighs and looked down at him as he touched her.

"You have very pretty skin, *mia* Angelina."

"*Grazie,* Dominic," she said. She cupped his jaw and ran her fingers over his face. "I love the feel of the stubble on your jaw."

"I have a heavy beard," he said, but his mind wasn't on this conversation. It was on the flesh he was slowly revealing as he drew the fabric of her blouse up her body.

The blouse was pretty and feminine and he found a zipper in the side of the garment and undid it. She stilled in his arms. Just hovering over him.

He slipped his hand into the gap made by the unfastened zipper. He felt the edge of her bra.

The fabric felt lacy as he caressed the fullness of her breast.

He pulled his hand out from under the blouse and caressed her through the fabric of her shirt. She shifted her shoulders, drawing his eyes to her hardened nipples. Placing his palm over the center of her breasts, he rotated his hands against her.

Her head fell back, revealing her long, pretty neck and he was transfixed by the sensual nature of this woman. He wanted her, but he felt a deep stab of lust that went beyond anything he'd experienced before.

"Dominic," she said. Just his name, spoken so deep and husky and so damned entrancing made him realize that any illusion of power he had was just that—an illusion. She was in charge. She was in control of him and his passion. And he wanted to wrest it back from her.

He leaned forward and kissed her neck. Nibbled his way from the base where her pulse pounded strongly. The scent of her perfume blended with a more natural essence of woman. He licked at her skin and felt her shiver in his arms.

"Dominic…"

"Sì?"

"I need more of you."

"How much more?" he asked. He wrapped his arms around her and spoke directly into her ear.

She shivered again. He felt her nipples tightened against the center of his palms. He moved them over her and she squirmed closer to him.

He bit lightly on the lobe of her ear, waiting for her reply. "Angelina?"

"*Sì*, Dominic?"

"How much more do you need?" he asked, tracing the shell of her ear with his tongue.

"All of you," she said.

She shifted on his lap, finding his erection with her center, and rocked her hips over him. He was tight and full and needed to feel her naked in his arms.

But he took his time, needing to wrest back control. And no matter how much he thought he might explode from the very thought of her hot core sliding over him, he was going to take his time.

He would seduce her in increments until she was a writhing mass and had no doubts who owned her body and soul.

He drew her blouse up over her arms and tossed it onto the floor. Her bra was pale blue lace with a pretty beige accent, but her breasts were all he wanted to see. Reaching behind her, he unhooked the bra, pulling the straps down her arms until she was finally naked from the waist up.

Angelina couldn't think as Dominic held her in his arms. No longer sad as she had been in the piazza earlier, she realized that Dominic was giving her a chance at something she'd always wanted.

Him.

She had been so afraid to take him. Afraid to believe he could be hers. And though he was only offering her six months, she knew that six months could change a person's life. And if she played her cards right…maybe, she and Dominic could have so much more. And even if they didn't, she knew she'd still cherish this time with him.

And since her parents' death, she'd had so little time in her life where she could just relax and enjoy a relationship. Dominic's caresses and his attention made her feel as if she were really alive. She reached up and touched his face, felt the shadow stubble on his jaw.

"What?"

She shook her head. How could she say that he made her want to start dreaming of a future again?

Made her want to believe in the dreams she'd abandoned to save her brother? "I'm just so glad to be here with you right now."

God, he was making her hot. His hands on her breasts were magic. He knew how to touch her so that she received the most pleasure from each caress. It had been a long time since she'd been in a man's arms. And Dominic had long been her fantasy man.

He nibbled on her neck and shoulders, holding her at his mercy. It didn't surprise her that Dominic would be so dominate. She dug her nails into his shoulders and leaned down, brushing against his chest. He felt so good. Her nipples were hard points when he pulled away from her.

"Do you like that, *mia?*"

"*Sì,* very much."

She closed her eyes and held her breath as he fondled her, running his finger over her nipple. She saw the absorption on his face as he brushed his finger back and forth until she bit her lower lip and shifted in his arms.

She moaned a sweet sound that he leaned down to capture. She tipped her head to the side so that she could open her mouth wider and let him all the way inside. She held his shoulders and moved on him, rubbing her core over his erection.

She needed to touch him, to feel his body against hers instead of the starched cotton of his Savile Row shirt. But he still held her wrists at the small of her back. Her breasts were thrust toward him, and watching the way he looked at her made her very proud of her less-than-perfect body.

Because she saw blatant desire in his eyes.

"Let me touch you," she said.

"Not yet."

He traced a path from her neck down her chest with his tongue. Circling the full globes of her breasts, narrowing the circle to come closer to her nipple but never touching it.

"Dominic…"

"*Sì,* Angelina?"

"Kiss me."

"Where?"

"There," she said, gesturing with her chin to her chest.

"Here?" he asked, sucking on the white fleshy part of her breast.

"No, Dominic."

"Here?" he asked, his breath moistening one nipple.

"Yes. Yes. Kiss me there."

He complied and she shook to her core as his

lips closed around her nipple. He suckled strongly on her and she shifted against him as she went completely liquid between her legs. She craved this man. Craved more of his touch.

She struggled to free her arms so she could pull him closer to her. "Let me go."

"Not...yet," he said.

He moved his mouth from one breast to the other, taking his time and nibbling against her skin. She felt overly sensitized by the warmth of his mouth against her.

She shifted on his lap, frustrated by her pants and his. Frustrated at the lack of control she had in this moment as Dominic continued to drive her slowly toward an orgasm. Her entire body felt so susceptible and she was out of control.

"Dominic, stop."

"Not yet, *mia* Angelina. I want to see you come for me."

"Not like this. You aren't even undressed."

"I don't have to be," he said.

She felt his free hand moving between their bodies, undoing the button of her pants and drawing down the zipper. His hand slipped inside and she shifted on her knees, lifting her body so that his fingers could reach to the very core of her.

"This doesn't feel like no," he said.

"It's not," she admitted. "I want you, Dominic."

"You are going to have me," he said. "But not until I've heard you scream with pleasure."

God, he hadn't been this hot since—never. This was more than just sex and it was important to him that he bring pleasure to Angelina. He wouldn't be satisfied with an orgasm until he knew he'd wrung out every ounce he could from her. He rubbed her nipple and she shivered in his arms. He pushed her back a little so he could see her. Her breasts were bare, nipples distended and begging for his mouth. He lowered his head and suckled.

He still held both of her wrists in one of his hands at the small of her back. The action kept her breasts thrust up toward him.

Her eyes were closed, her hips moving subtly against his hand, which he'd cupped around her body. He teased her with his finger through her panties. The humid warmth of her body branded him as he continued to stroke her. He blew on her nipple and watched as gooseflesh spread down her body.

He loved the way she reacted to his mouth on her breast. Her nipples were so sensitive he was pretty sure he could bring her to an orgasm just from touching her there.

"When you come for me, Angelina, that will seal our deal. There will be no backing down. You will be mine."

He bit carefully at the creamy skin of her chest. "Do you agree?"

"*Sì,* Dominic."

"Say it," he said.

"I'll be yours."

He groaned at the sound of her agreeing that she belonged to him.

He kept kissing and rubbing, suckling her nipples, trying to quench his thirst, until she rocked her hips harder against his hand. He was straining inside his trousers. He had her hot wetness against his palm, and his hot erection against the other side of his hand.

It was one of the most sensual things he'd ever felt. He pulled his hand free of her pants and then lifted his hips. He so wanted to feel her on him. He wanted to do away with the layers of clothing between them. He needed to feel her long sexy legs wrapped around him until they were truly one person.

He bit carefully on her tender, aroused nipple.

She moaned and shifted against him, her hips rocking over him.

"I need more."

"More of what?"

"Your hand, Dominic," she said.

"Beg me," he said.

She opened her eyes and looked up at him. She was completely at his mercy. "Please touch me again."

"Like this?" he asked, slipping his hand back into her pants, rubbing her again through the crotch of her panties.

"No." She shook her head.

He stopped caressing her. "You don't like that?"

She rocked her hips over his hand. "More. Please, Dominic, give me more."

He pulled the crotch of her panties to one side and slid one finger against the warmth of her core. She moaned.

"Is that what you wanted?"

"Oh yes."

He traced the opening of her body with his finger and then slipped the tip into her. She tightened around him, rearing up on her knees and then sinking back down.

"Oh, Dominic."

He liked the sound of his name on her lips when passion overcame her. He added a second finger and she rubbed herself against him again.

This time he pressed his thumb to her and rubbed up and down, sending her soaring. He felt the climax rip through her body as she screamed and convulsed in his arms.

He brought his mouth down on hers and drank the sounds of her passion. Wrapping himself in her ardor as she came.

He rocked her until her orgasm faded. Letting go of her wrists, he stroked her back and kept kissing her. Holding her close, her bare breasts brushed against his chest. Now he was ready to take her. He was so hard he thought he'd die if he didn't get inside her.

He glanced down at her and saw she was watching him. The fire in her eyes made his entire body tight with anticipation. He gently pushed her back so that she stood before him. Getting to her own feet, he stripped her pants off.

"Are you on the pill?" he asked.

"No," she said.

"Damn."

"I'm sorry."

"Don't be," he said, framing her face and kissing her. "I think I have a condom with me."

He took the condom from his pocket and then removed his pants before sitting back down. "Come here."

She climbed on his lap once again. Unbuttoning his shirt, she pushed it off his shoulders. "You are very sexy, Dominic."

She traced his muscles and her touch was almost too much. He quickly put on the condom.

"Are you ready for me now?" she asked teasingly, her hand going to his erection. She caressed him and then moved her hand up his abdomen. Her hands were small and infinitely exciting. He wanted to let her touch him all night, but he was too near the edge and he wanted to be inside her when he went over.

"Ah, Angelina," he said. "You are so tempting."

"Am I?" she asked. He noticed a slight hesitation in her voice.

"You have no idea," he said.

"I'm glad. You tempt me, too. Make love to me, Dominic. I want to experience every bit of passion you have."

He shifted his hands, gripping her thighs so that he could enter her. Her hands fluttered between them and their eyes met.

He held her hips steady and entered her slowly, thrusting deeply. Her eyes widened with each inch he gave her. She clutched at his shoulders as he started thrusting harder. Her eyes were half closed and she was biting her lower lip.

He caught one of her nipples in his teeth, scraping very gently, and felt her start to tighten around him. Her hips moved faster, demanding more, but he kept the pace slow and steady. Wanting her to come again before he did.

He suckled her nipple and rotated his hips to catch her pleasure point with each thrust. Soon he felt her hands clench his hair as she threw her head back, her climax ripping through her.

He varied his thrusts to find a rhythm that would draw out the tension at the base of his spine. Leaning back against the couch, he tipped her hips to give him deeper access. Then she scraped her nails down his chest. Blood roared in his ears and he called her name as he came.

Wrapping his arms around her, he held her close. He'd gotten more than he expected. He had wanted revenge, but now there was so much more between them.

"Dominic?"

"Hmm?"

"Thank you."

"For what?" he asked.

"For everything."

Her thanks made him feel very uncomfortable. He knew his lovemaking had nothing to do with vengeance but hearing her sincere gratitude made him feel…

Well, made him *feel.* He'd been careful to never let a woman evoke any emotions in him since… No, he wouldn't go there.

He lifted Angelina to her feet. "I've got to clean up. Where's the bathroom?"

"Through there," she said, gesturing toward the darkened doorway to the left.

Walking down the hall, he glanced back to see her standing in the middle of the room, naked and vulnerable. He could not allow himself to fall under her spell—he had to maintain emotional distance. She was now his mistress—that was all she could ever be.

He like pushing her to her limits and each time she hesitated he knew he was finding another place where she was afraid to let him go. In this case it was that fragility that she revealed in her nudity.

He never would have guessed that Angelina

had any issues with her body given the confidence with which she carried herself. He'd realized when Ian told him Angelina was the one selling company secrets that he didn't know everything about her—but he'd never understood how complicated she really was.

"You're staring at me," she said.

"I am."

He drew one finger down the center of her body. Her curves were full and tempting. So soft compared to the hardness of his own frame.

"What are you thinking?" he asked.

"That I wished we had come together because of our mutual attraction and not because of my misdeeds."

"I asked you out tonight before I knew the truth. You declined," he pointed out.

"Yes, you did. But I knew you were going to find out about me and I couldn't go out with you with that lie between us. Whatever else you might think about me, please believe I never wanted to hurt you."

"Then why *did* you lie?"

"I felt trapped," she said.

"Tell me more about your brother," he said, moving to sit at the head of the bed.

Five

Angelina stood in her living room for about a minute before she heard the water come on in the bathroom. Realizing she didn't want to be standing here naked when Dominic came back into the room she reached for her clothes but heard Dominic's footsteps behind her before she had put anything on. She glanced over at him. He was naked and very male. She couldn't help but notice the way he filled the small living room with his presence.

Oh, man, she had it bad. She wanted nothing more than to cross the room and wrap her arms around his waist and feel his arms around her.

She wanted to take comfort from his body and offer him the comfort of hers. And she had no idea if that was something he was interested in.

Dominic looked down at his watch and then back at her, giving her her answer. He was leaving. And somehow tomorrow morning she'd have to figure out how to face him and how to make this relationship…this arrangement…work for both of them.

"I need to get my robe if we're going to talk," she said.

"Of course."

She walked past him, and maintaining her cool was the hardest thing she had ever done. Because she wasn't cool. She couldn't be nonchalant.

Hold it together, she told herself. Get used to it. This was going to be her life—for the next six months at least.

She fumbled for her robe and pulled it on. The ivory-colored, silk-lined robe was too heavy for this spring evening, but it was the only one she had and it had been a gift from her grandmother. And when she pulled the sides closed and tied the sash at her waist she felt as if her grandmother were giving her a hug.

She closed her eyes and drew strength from the

woman who was long gone, but had always been Angelina's ally.

"Angelina?"

"*Sì,* Dominic," she said, turning to see him standing in her doorway.

He'd put on his pants but left his shirt off. "Do you want me to leave?"

"Don't you want to go?" she asked.

His eyes narrowed and he crossed his arms over his chest then leaned against the doorjamb. "No," he said.

"Then stay."

She could say no more than that. She knew she had to keep her emotional distance. Falling for Dominic, letting him know that was a possibility was pure foolishness.

"Can I ask you something?"

"Yes."

"Why would you settle for this kind of relationship with me when you could have something real with another woman?"

"This feels real to me," he said, walking into the room.

He sat down on the edge of her bed and then snagged her wrist, drawing her close to him. "Doesn't this feel real to you?"

She swallowed hard. She wasn't explaining this the right way. She wanted…she wanted him to say that there was more between them than an arrangement, but there was no way that was going to happen. She knew that wasn't possible—not yet. Maybe never. She'd used him, and now it was his turn to use her.

"I guess so."

He pulled her even closer, wrapped his arms around her waist and rested his head on her shoulder. The move was unexpected and she didn't know what it meant. But she realized that thinking and analyzing this wasn't going to bring her the answers she sought. Not tonight.

She wrapped her arms around him and held him close for a few minutes. "I'm sorry for betraying you."

"I know you are."

"What are you going to do next?"

"I'm going to trap Barty Eastburn and make sure that bastard never steals from anyone again."

She nodded. "You'll need my help."

"Yes. Ian is going to come up with a plan and we will be discussing it tomorrow."

Dominic let go of her and stood. He pulled back the duvet on her bed and motioned for her to get in. She climbed onto the bed, though she knew her robe was going to be too hot to sleep in.

He took off his pants and she had a chance to just stare at his almost naked body. The boxer briefs he wore clung to his buttocks and thighs as he turned away from her. When he turned back she stared at his body. He was toned and muscled and she wanted nothing more than to explore his form.

"Like what you see?" he asked.

She gave him an embarrassed grin. But Dominic was at home in his skin and held his hands out to his sides. "Look all you want."

"I want to touch you, too," she said.

"If you're good, that might be arranged." He sat down on the bed next to her.

"What constitutes good?"

"Lose that robe and I'll tell you."

She loosened the sash and had the robe halfway off before she remembered she wasn't drop-dead gorgeous like Dominic Moretti. But by the time the thought entered her head it was too late. Dominic had taken the robe and tossed it on the floor.

She sat there in a pool of light from her bedside lamp, naked and vulnerable, and for the first time in her life, that didn't bother her.

Dominic knew spending the night with Angelina was a mistake, but he'd be unable to walk away when he'd seen those wounded chocolate-colored eyes of hers.

She was easily the sexiest woman he'd seen in years. And a part of that sexiness came from the total unawareness she had of her own attractiveness. There was a guileless way about her that drew him.

A part of him feared that it was all a lie—she had been a spy. But tonight—just for tonight—that didn't matter. He wanted to enjoy every second he could with her until the sun came up and they were forced to move on to the role of mistress and master.

"That's very good, Angelina. Now lie back against the pillows."

She curled on her side, drawing the sheet up to her breasts and wrapping one arm around his waist. He put his arm around her shoulder. This quiet moment of holding one another had nothing to do with revenge or any kind of arrangement. Was she his Achilles' heel? Was this how Lorenzo had found himself cursed—falling for some of this quiet comfort in a woman's arms?

Dominic had no answers. He only knew that he

needed this tonight. That making love to Angelina had taken the edge off his anger.

"What do you want to know about Renni?" she asked, running her fingers over his chest.

"If I offered him a job…would he take it?"

She sat up, her hand square in the middle of his chest. "Would you do that?"

"I'm thinking about it."

She kissed him, taking her time. And when she lifted her head from his, he felt like a different man.

This relationship with Angelina was going to be a double-edged sword. She was going to always feel grateful to him and he was going to…he was going to stop acting like a sap and remember that what they had was nothing more than a six-month affair.

Once his brother wrapped up the Vallerio problem and got the rights to that name back, there'd be nothing standing in the way of Moretti Motors making a full comeback. Over the last few years they'd surpassed what *Nono* had done during his storied run as CEO, and now Dominic had his eye on setting a new standard of excellence.

"What are you thinking?" Angelina asked. "You looked so fierce just now."

"I was thinking about Moretti Motors and how close I came to letting all the success I worked so hard for slip through my fingers."

"And that you'll never do it again?" she asked.

"Damned straight."

Ian was already in the office when Dominic arrived the next morning. He'd left Angelina's apartment early, before she was fully awake. He had a list of things that he needed to get finished before he could start thinking about setting Angelina up as his mistress.

"I need ten minutes before we start," Dominic said to Ian.

"Not a problem. I'll go give Tony a hard time about cars."

"Thanks."

Ian left and Dominic sat down in the leather chair that had been his grandfather's. He took a minute to jot down the arrangement he'd offered Angelina and then clarified some points before contacting his solicitor. He knew the man would make sure Dominic was covered in all regards to this relationship.

He typed a quick e-mail to Bruno Marcelli, his solicitor, and then sat back in his chair. He wanted some formal guidelines set up for his relationship with Angelina, to protect him because he was in danger of forgetting that she wasn't more than a mistress. He also needed to find a place for her to live.

He rang Antonio's office and Ian returned to his office a few minutes later.

"Have you had a thought about how we can get enough on Barty Eastburn to have him arrested?" Dominic asked as Ian took a seat in the guest chair.

"Yes, but first I wanted to talk to you about this idea you have of not prosecuting Angelina De Luca."

"I've made my mind up, Ian." Dominic had called Ian first thing.

Ian shook his head. "I don't think you're being smart about this."

"Duly noted. Now talk to me about Eastburn."

"Dominic—"

"I'm not going to change my mind, Ian. I've taken care of the problem with Angelina and it won't be an issue."

"How?"

"How what?"

"How have you taken care of it?"

"By offering her an alternate arrangement. She will even help us trap Barty if need be."

"Okay, fine. Near as I can tell, Eastburn is hoping to muck up Moretti Motors' reacquisition of the Vallerio name for the new roadster. My guy inside ESP said they want to bump back the release date of the car, giving ESP Motors the chance to get their roadster to market before you."

"Like hell. I'll sue him if he tries to use the engine we developed."

"Bruno Marcelli has a team already on it. Antonio is working with the legal team to make sure that ESP is stopped from releasing any cars until we can ascertain that they haven't been made using Moretti Motors' proprietary information."

"Good. I will talk to Antonio when you and I are done here," Dominic said. "What do we need to do now?"

"We have to get Eastburn on record asking for someone to bring corporate documents from your office. Will De Luca do it?"

"Yes, she will," Dominic said. Angelina would do whatever he asked. That was one of the things he'd discussed with her last night and that he'd had Bruno put into their agreement.

"Great. Then all we need is to find out how he

usually contacts her. When will she be in the office this morning?"

"She should be here now. She wouldn't have disturbed me since the door is closed."

Ian nodded. "If you're ready to bring her in, I recommend we do that now."

Dominic nodded. He lifted the handset on his phone and hit the intercom button.

"*Sì,* Dominic?" Her voice came through the line.

"I need you in here, Angelina."

"I'll be right in."

When he hung up, Ian was watching him. "Are you involved with her?" his friend asked.

"That's not pertinent to this investigation," he replied.

"I'm asking as your friend, Dom. I have never known you to get involved with anyone you work with."

"This is different. We have an arrangement."

Ian started to say something else, but the door opened and Angelina walked in. It was impossible to look at her curvy frame clad in a slim-fitting shirtdress without remembering what she'd looked like this morning, naked in bed.

His erection stirred and he knew now why he'd

always resisted getting involved with a woman he worked with. This was going to be damned uncomfortable until he got through the intense period of wanting her.

What if that never happened?

"You asked to see me?"

"Yes, please have a seat," Dominic said. "Ian has a few questions for you about how you passed information to Barty Eastburn."

She flushed a little. "I usually got a call from Renni."

"Who is Renni?" Ian asked.

"My brother. He had some gambling debts that Barty took care of. So Renni calls me when he has had to borrow more money from Barty."

"Does Barty ever call you directly?"

"Sometimes. Or he has me call him."

"Would you be willing to tape your phone calls with him?"

"Of course she will," Dominic said.

"We need her consent, Dom. Without it, the courts will say she was coerced."

"I will do it, Signore Stark."

Angelina looked up at Dominic before she added, "I will do whatever it takes to make this right."

Six

"Signore Stark, I am supposed to go to London next week to meet with Barty. I was going to tell him I'm through passing him information," Angelina said.

She was trying to concentrate on the meeting, but instead she was swamped with images of her and Dominic from the night before. It was hard to look at Dominic and not want to be back in his arms.

Of course the way he was looking at her, totally impersonal, made it a bit easier. But that also made her nervous. What did he expect from her?

"That's good. When are you supposed to meet him?"

"Next Wednesday. Dominic is scheduled to go to the F1 race in Catalonia, Spain."

"Good. So we can set up this meeting with Barty. I will follow you to London," Ian said.

"I don't like it, I should be there," Dominic said.

"You can't be, Dom. If you aren't where you are supposed to be, Eastburn will suspect you're on to him."

"I agree with Signore Stark," Angelina said. "Barty isn't a very trusting man. He always has me followed when I leave a meeting with him."

"How do you know?" Dominic asked.

"I saw his man," Angelina said. She'd never admit it to these men, but it had scared her at first. She didn't know what Barty's man would do to her. And for all that she was confident of herself and her abilities to take care of herself, the man was so tall and broad, she knew she wouldn't stand a chance if he attacked her.

"Are you sure he was following you?"

"Yes, and it's the same man everytime. The one time Renni was with me, the first time, he said that the man—Patrick, he called him—worked for Barty."

"So the man's name is Patrick?" Dominic asked.

"*Sì.*"

"Is this the man you call Patrick?" Ian asked, pulling a photo from a manila folder.

She looked at a photo of herself and Barty. Ian tapped the man sitting at a table behind them.

"Yes, that's him," Angelina said. "How did you discover it was me?"

"I followed the trail of paperwork," Ian said. "Dom was very good at limiting who had the information, and the two men we thought were suspects never left Milan and never delivered information anywhere."

She noted that Dominic's eyes narrowed as Ian spoke about her betraying him. She wondered if being his mistress was really going to be recompense enough. She suspected it wasn't and that really upset her.

"Well, I don't know who Patrick is to Eastburn, but he seems to have his fingers in a lot of pies," Angelina said.

"I suspected as much. I'm going to run him through a few of my databases. If he's involved in organized crime…well, I have another client who will be interested in that."

"What will we do next week?" she asked Ian.

She didn't care about anything but making things up to Dominic.

"You will do what you've always done with Barty. I will follow and record the meeting. Does he search you when you arrive?"

"No. At least he never has."

"He must be very confident that you won't betray him," Dominic said, a tinge of anger in his voice.

"I think it is more that he knows he holds all the cards."

"Not anymore," Dominic said. "What's the plan, Ian?"

"I want Angelina to wear a wire so we can record the conversation. I have a very sophisticated one that I can embed in a brooch."

"I can do that. What do I say to him?"

"Just let him do the talking. Have you ever suggested information you can give him?"

"No. He's always known exactly what he wants and asks me for it."

"Good. That's all I really need. Together with the photos we should have enough proof."

Angelina nodded. "I told my brother he had to come back to Milan this time. I really was trying to find a way to stop having to give Barty information."

"Why didn't you go to the police or to Dominic?" Ian asked.

She looked at both men. "I didn't know what to say to the police. Renni has a criminal record. I couldn't chance getting him in trouble, maybe have him go back to jail. I didn't want that. He's all the family I have."

"That's understandable," Dominic said. "But why not talk to me?"

"Everyone looks to you to solve their problems and I didn't want to be just one more person in a long line," she said.

"That's a lame excuse," Dominic said.

"Yes, it is. The truth is I'm used to fixing my own problems. It never occurred to me to turn to you."

"I guess stealing from me seemed different to you," he said with a bitter edge to his voice.

She felt a sting of tears at his words. "I never thought of it that way, but I can see that you're right. Stealing from you wasn't the right thing to do. But, unlike the great Dominic Moretti, I'm only human and infinitely fallible."

"The important thing is that we're moving on now. You're making reparations to Dominic and making amends by helping us trap Barty," Ian said.

She could tell by Dominic's lack of reaction that he didn't think there was anything good about this situation. She realized that she'd given herself to a man who didn't want anything from her beyond what their agreement stated.

Suddenly she was very unsure that she could turn this negative into a positive. That she could find a way to make Dominic Moretti forgive her for her crimes. Because she saw the seeds of a man she could really like.

After Ian and Angelina left, Dominic thought back to his earlier reaction. Perhaps he'd been too harsh with her, but hearing Angelina talk about meeting with his enemy had been more than he could take. And he *was* human, despite what she seemed to think.

He needed to be alone. He was going to take one of his Moretti coupes to the track outside the city and drive it as fast as he could. Anything to get away from this mess and clear his head.

He knew he was making mistakes with Angelina, which was one thing he couldn't abide.

There was a knock on his door. "Enter."

Angelina stood there with her notepad in one

hand and a very hesitant look on her face. "Do you want to go over your schedule for the day?"

No, what he wanted was to reaffirm that she was his mistress. That her loyalty was owed only to him.

"Close the door and lock it, Angelina, and then come over here."

She swallowed and tipped her head to one side. "What do you have in mind?"

"Whatever I want, remember? That is our arrangement."

Angelina locked the door and then leaned back against it. "I know I said…anything you wanted, but I never expected you to ask me for anything personal here at the office."

"Neither did I. But I want you and you are my mistress, aren't you, Angelina?"

"Yes, I am," she said, straightening from the wall. "Do you want me, Dominic?"

"More than I should," he said, giving her the truth. She was a courageous woman and he realized part of why he needed to make love to her now was the fact that she had placed herself in danger. The men who were after her brother wouldn't hesitate to hurt her.

"Come to me," he said.

She moved slowly toward him with sensual grace, the ruffled hem of her dress bouncing lightly around her thighs. He stood and crossed the small space between them in two long strides. Sweeping her up in his arms, he carried her to his desk.

Her mouth opened under his and he told himself to take it slow. That if he was going to retain any objectivity where she was concerned, he really needed to keep his cool, but that simply wasn't possible. She was pure feminine temptation. He slid his hands down her back, down to the end of her dress, and slipped his hand underneath. He felt the silk of her hose and then just bare skin.

He set her on her feet next to the wide mahogany desk. He wanted, needed, to keep things light between them. To make the sex between them something of a game so that he didn't forget to keep his objectivity and so that she didn't forget that this was temporary. That they were lovers only until the six months was up.

"Do you like it when I tell you what to do?" he asked, coming up behind her. He wrapped his arms around her waist and drew her back against his body.

She turned her head to the side, resting it on his shoulder, and he felt a curious emotion inside him. An emotion that had nothing to do with lust. For a moment he tightened his arms around her, wanting to bury his face in her thick hair.

He wanted to pretend that her betrayal didn't matter. That it didn't matter that she'd spent time with his bitter rival Barty Eastburn. That it didn't matter if he fell for her because he was no longer a man cursed by past generations.

But all of that did matter. "Angelina?"

"*Sì*, Dominic?"

"Do you like it when I tell you what to do?" he asked again.

She glanced up at him, a slight blush coloring her face. "I do. There is a certain freedom and being able to act without…"

She trailed off and he realized what she was going to say. "Without taking responsibility?"

"Yes. I'm sorry, that's not fair to you."

"In this case it's perfectly fair. You have agreed to give your body to me whenever I ask. And I have agreed to give you pleasure until you forget your name."

"Wow, that's what you agreed to?" she asked, a teasing note in her voice.

"*Sì.*"

She smiled at him, making him very aware that

she hadn't smiled at all in the meeting with Ian. In fact, this was the first time today he'd seen genuine happiness on her face. And he was the one who caused it. He'd made her happy.

It shouldn't matter to him; she was only his mistress. But it did matter. He stopped thinking and started to feel.

"Bend forward, place your hands on the desk," he said.

She did as he said, bracing her hands awkwardly on the smooth surface. "Like this?"

"Just like that. Wait, are you wearing panties?"

She flushed. "Yes! Or course."

He bit the inside of his mouth to keep from smiling. "Take them off."

She straightened and turned to face him. She lifted her skirt to her waist revealing thigh-high sheer hose and a tiny pair of race-car-red panties. Slowly she took the sides of her panties and drew them down her legs.

When she reached her knees she pushed them to the floor and delicately stepped out of the undergarment. She started to lower her skirt, but he stopped her.

"Leave your skirt up and turn back around."

She hesitated and he saw the vulnerability in

her eyes. He kissed her. He didn't draw her into his arms but took her mouth with his and reassured her the only way he could. If she didn't like this, he would stop and just make love to her on the leather guest chair.

She grasped his shoulders and pulled herself closer to him. Her head tilted to give them both deeper access to each other's mouths. And once again he was struck by the fact that where this woman was concerned he had no discipline. She'd undermined him again. Right now all he wanted to do was free his erection and take her.

He took her hips in his hands. Her butt was firm and smooth and he caressed the furrow between her cheeks.

She swiveled her hips against his touch, and he slipped his touch deeper until he caressed that slit between her legs. She was wet and hot with her desire. He stroked the edge of her femininity, circling the edge of her body with his finger. She said his name on a long sigh.

"Yes?"

"You make me so hot," she said. "No other has ever taken over my body the way you do."

"Good. Unbutton your blouse," he said. "I want to see your breasts."

He kept his hand between her legs as she slowly undid the buttons. The blouse fell open down her shoulders, over her arms.

Her bra matched the red panties at his feet. It was a demi-bra with cups that only covered the bottom half of her breasts. They looked delicate and tempting. The lace detail was black and a contrast to her creamy skin.

"Turn around again," he said, his own voice husky and deep.

She did as he said and leaned on the desk, thrusting her butt back toward him. He leaned over her, his big body completely blanketing hers. He bent his legs so his erection rubbed at her core. Through the fabric of his pants he felt her heat.

The top of her blouse almost fell off of her body. And from his angle looking over her shoulder, he could only see the tops of her breasts, and the barest hint of the rosy flesh of her nipples. He reached up one hand and drew the lace down away from her nipple, completely exposing it.

He ran the tip of one fingertip around her aroused flesh. She trembled in his arms. He undid the front clasp of her bra and brushed the cups away. He took one of her nipples between his fingers and pinched her lightly. She shifted against him. Her hips thrust back against him and she shifted until her core rubbed over the ridge of his hardness.

She tried to turn in his arms, but he held her in place. "Dominic…"

"Yes?"

"I want to touch you."

He wanted that, too. But he knew if he felt her fingers on his chest or on his erection, he would be inside her and this moment would end. And he wasn't ready for that yet.

"No," he said, growling deep in his throat. He leaned forward to nibble at the elegant length of her neck. He ran his tongue down the side of it until she shivered with pleasure. He reached between her legs to find her nether lips. Stroking her, he kept his touch light until she went up on her tiptoes and thrust her hips back into him.

Then he lightly traced her. She screamed his name as she tried to turn in his arms. But he held her still, his hands on her body.

He felt her heart beating frantically in her chest. Her hips moved urgently trying to find the pinnacle of her release. He drove her relentlessly toward it but stopped before she climaxed, holding her at the edge of sensation so that she would enjoy it more later.

"Do you like that?"

"Yes. Yes, I do, Dominic, but I need more."

"More of this?" he asked, scraping his finger over her nipple.

She shook her head. He took his hand from her breast and unzipped his pants, freeing his erection.

"More of this?" he asked, leaning forward to speak directly into her ear as he pushed one finger into her body. She tightened on him and he felt the tiny contractions as she began to orgasm. He quickly pulled his finger back out and she moaned at the loss.

"Yes. That."

He pulled her to him and lifted her slightly so that her buttocks were nestled against his abdomen. He leaned over her, bracing his hands on the desk next to hers, and let her feel his chest against her back. Blood roared in his ear. He was so hard, so full right now.

He caressed her creamy thighs. *Dios,* she was soft, something he hadn't forgotten from the first time he'd had her. She moaned as he neared her center and then sighed when he brushed his fingertips against her humid warmth.

He turned his head to watch her as he tested her

readiness, this time with the tip of himself. Her eyes were heavy lidded. She bit down on her lower lip and he felt the minute movements of her hips as she tried to take him deeper, to make him enter her. But he held his hips steady and waited, prolonging the moment until he couldn't take it anymore.

He needed her *now.* Their naked loins pressed together and he shook under the impact. Naked loins…dammit, he needed a condom.

He reached into his pocket and pulled out the packet he'd put there earlier. He donned it quickly and then came back to her. She'd stood there waiting for him. Her hips lifted slightly and he knew that she was as hot for him as he was for her.

He had to have her. *Now.* He cupped both of her breasts in his hands, plucking at her aroused nipples. He adjusted his stance, bending his knees and positioning himself, and then entered her with one long, hard stroke.

She moaned his name and her head fell forward leaving the curve of her neck open and vulnerable to him. He bit softly at her neck and felt the reaction all the way to his toes when she squirmed in his arms and thrust her hips back toward him.

A tingling started in the base of his spine and

he knew his climax was close. But he wasn't going without Angelina. He wanted her with him. He caressed her stomach and her breasts. Whispered erotic words of praise and longing in her ears.

She moved more frantically in his arms and he thrust deeper with each stroke. Breathing out through his mouth, he tried to hold back the inevitable. He slid one hand down her abdomen, through the slick folds of her sex. Finding her center, he stroked the aroused flesh with an up-and-down movement. She continued to writhe in his arms no closer to her climax than before.

He circled that aroused bit of flesh between her legs with his forefinger, then scraped it very carefully. She screamed his name and tightened around him. Penetrating her as deeply as he could, he bit down on the back of her neck and came long and hard, emptying himself into her body.

He wasn't cold or alone anymore, he acknowledged, and that scared him more than he wanted to admit. More than he would ever admit. Because Moretti's legacy was built for a solitary man and he wasn't about to give up his heritage for Angelina. No matter how right she felt in his arms.

Seven

She was damp between her legs and her entire body was still trembling from the incredible orgasm she'd just had in his arms when Dominic pulled away and gave her such an odd look it felt like he was a stranger.

"You may use my washroom if you need to," he said.

She nodded and bent to pick up her panties. She pulled her clothes on and walked away from him on shaking legs.

The intimacy of what had just transpired between them had forced them further apart rather than bringing them closer together. She closed the door and avoided looking at herself in the mirror.

She'd thought that starting this affair with Dominic was a way to stay. The obvious one of staying out of jail. And, perhaps she hoped to get a little closer.

And she wondered if the bad luck she'd always had with men was going to dominate this relationship, too. She longed to have a man fall for her and treat her like a princess.

Being treated like a sexy lady was fine, too, but as she wrapped her arms around her waist she realized it also left her feeling hollow.

She heard the outer door of Dominic's office open and she wondered if he'd left. She hastily cleaned up and refastened her clothing. A glance in the mirror told her what she already sensed. She looked as though she was about to cry.

She refused to shed one tear. She'd made the choice that had led to this and she really needed to own up to her actions. And she had enjoyed the lovemaking with Dominic at his desk. His desk.

Oh my God, she thought.

She was entering an entirely new phase in her life…she had to let go of the past and of dreams that she'd clung to like a girl. She was a woman—with a woman's mistakes and experiences behind her. And if she had a chance at ever getting Dominic to see her as something more than a mistress, she had to start taking more control in their relationship.

She'd let Renni use her because she loved him and she had the bad feeling that if she wasn't careful she would let Dominic do the same thing.

She exited the washroom to find Dominic and Ian both in his office.

"Are you okay?" Dominic asked.

She nodded. "Yes. I'll go back to my desk now unless you need me?"

"That's fine. Ian wants to go over the arrangements for you both to head to London. He will be out in a few minutes."

She walked out of his office, feeling as if she'd never get back to her desk, but then she was there. She sat down on her chair and really had to fight to keep her equilibrium.

The phone rang and she answered it, glad for the distraction. "Signore Moretti's office, this is Angelina."

"*Ciao,* Angelina. This is Bruno Marcelli, Dominic's solicitor."

"He's in a meeting right now, can I take a message?"

"Yes, please tell him that the arrangement he asked me to draw up is ready for his review. I'm going to fax it over now," Bruno said.

"Is it for the Vallerio agreement?" she asked.

"No, it's a personal matter. In fact, it involves you, Ms. De Luca. The fax I'm sending is for you," he said.

"Is this regarding my personal arrangement with Dominic?" she asked.

"Indeed. Signore Moretti has authorized me to offer you the services of one of our solicitors and my associate Signore Lunestri will be contacting you later today to discuss it. There will be no charge to you for this service."

"*Grazie,* Signore Marcelli."

"You're welcome. *Ciao.*"

She hung up the phone and a minute later heard the ring of the fax machine. She stood and went over to the machine, wanting to remove the papers from the tray before anyone else came into the office. It was a private machine, but being Dominic's mistress and having others know it wasn't what she wanted.

This wasn't turning out the way she wanted it

to. And she remembered the vow she'd just made to herself in Dominic's washroom. The promise that she'd take control of this. She pulled the papers off the machine and read them over carefully.

In her mind she started to change the entire way she'd been viewing her affair with Dominic. She had felt guilty for her actions in the entire corporate espionage thing, but she realized she had to let go of her guilt.

Dominic wasn't going to forget it and she never would, either, but it could no longer be the focus of her every action around him.

She took a pen and started making notes on the document, which was very generous. She was sure that Dominic didn't expect her to turn down his offer of a new wardrobe or an apartment, or the many other things he could give her, but she knew, deep inside, that she didn't want *things.*

She wanted Dominic Moretti, and the only way to win him was to make him realize she wasn't like every other woman he'd known.

The new penthouse apartment that Dominic had selected for her was large with an entire wall of windows overlooking the city of Milan. It was quiet and felt empty despite the fact that it was filled with sleek ultramodern furniture. In the two weeks since she'd signed the agreement to become Dominic's mistress, she'd realized that living with him was going to be a challenge.

She'd gone to London to meet Barty wearing the brooch and bringing the false information with her. Ian had been in place, and they had been ready to entrap him, but instead Patrick had shown up to retrieve the information.

So she'd had to leave Renni in London to continue his gambling in case Barty was onto the trap they were trying to set. Ian had worked out the details and Angelina had simply gone along with them. Deciding to let herself be a pawn. It was what she'd been in this mess from the beginning.

She'd made a concerted effort to try to make him see her as more than a mistress.

Like when she'd made them a picnic lunch and convinced him to leave the office for an hour. They'd driven out of the city and had a quiet meal. They'd talked about books and travel, and she'd realized they had a lot in common on a very basic level. She'd mentioned that she loved finding out the history of old buildings. And Dominic had confessed he did the same, but with cars.

The next day he'd given her a book on architecture in Milan, and then he'd taken her that evening to one of his favorite old buildings. They'd explored the old stone facades and talked. Just talked. Angelina hadn't realized how long it had been since someone had listened to her and shared an interest with her that wasn't related to work or money.

Though there were times when she felt she'd succeeded, when she looked around this ultramodern place that he'd outfitted for them, she felt as though they were nothing but sex partners. He had to know that this place wasn't…wasn't the kind of place she could picture herself living in.

Was she giving him too much credit by suspecting that he had done it for her? She knew he must have some clue that she was falling for him. It was hard not to tell him how much she cared about him in the middle of the night when he made love to her. Their evenings together weren't like the obviously sexual games he played at the office or in the showroom or even in the new Moretti Motors Vallerio Roadster.

"Do you like it?" he asked, coming to stand behind her.

"Do you?" she asked. She'd been very careful

to keep things between them stress free. She wanted Dominic to realize that they could have a longer relationship and to be honest she was trying to be exactly what he wanted. She was adventurous in the bedroom and tried to be sweet out of it.

"I've just seen it."

She shook her head. "Dominic, didn't you approve the furniture in here?"

"No."

"Why not? You told me you were buying this place, not renting it."

"It will only be my home for the next five months or so. The furnishings don't matter too much to me—except the bedroom. I did ask for a king-size bed so we will both have enough room."

"Do you do this for all your mistresses?" she asked.

"You are different," he said.

She smiled at him as she felt tears sting the back of her eyes. "Thank you."

"You are very welcome. Now let's explore the place. Check out the bed."

She followed him into the kitchen, thinking that he always made her feel like the sexiest woman alive even though she was nothing close to it.

There was something about having a man want her the way Dominic did that took her breath away. Her mobile rang when they entered the kitchen area. "Do you mind if I get that?"

"Who is it?"

She glanced at the caller ID. "I'm not sure. It's an out-of-country code."

"Don't forget to use the recording button that Ian installed on your phone."

"I will," she said.

She hit the button to answer the call and record it. "*Ciao,* this is Angelina."

"*Ciao,* Ange."

"Renni, how are you?"

"Good. I'm calling you because I need a favor."

"What do you need?"

"Do you remember Jillian Stiles? I dated her two years ago?"

"Not really," she said. Her brother went through women very quickly. "Why?"

"She's going to be in Milan next month, and since you aren't going to be living in your place I thought maybe she could use it," he said.

She'd let Renni know when they'd planned for

him to come to Milan—before Barty's behavior had changed their plans.

"I don't know. Let me think about it and I'll call you back."

"She needs to know soon," Renni said.

"Why can't she stay with you?" Angelina asked.

"She'll be coming with me from London, and I've got a new job now," he said, referring to the job that Dominic had gotten him in the Moretti Motors plant. "And if she stays with me I will not go to work. I'll stay home and play with her. I don't want to let you down, Ang."

How was she supposed to say no to that? "Oh—"

"What does your brother want?" Dominic asked, putting his hand over the mouthpiece of the phone.

"To let his ex-girlfriend stay at my place next month."

"Why?"

"So she can save money," Angelina said.

"Are you going to do it?" Dominic asked.

"Probably. Renni doesn't want to take a chance on messing up at his new job. I think he took your warning to heart."

"I'm glad to hear it. If you let her stay there, will your stuff be safe?" Dominic asked.

"I don't know."

Dominic looked at her for a minute. "We'll move your stuff here before she comes. That way you know she won't go through anything."

"I...okay."

"Finish up so we can go and check out the king-size bed."

He removed his hand from the mouthpiece and she told Renni that his friend could use her place. Dominic had gone into the living room and she stood in the doorway of the kitchen area watching him. And thinking that there was a lot more to him than he wanted the world to see.

Dominic wanted Angelina all to himself, which had been one of the reasons he'd offered her brother a job. Now she'd have freedom from having to worry over the boy. And despite the fact that Renni was only two years younger than Angelina, he was still a boy.

"I'm sorry about that."

"It's nothing. I'm glad that he is taking his job seriously," Dominic said.

"Me, too. I was afraid that he'd do something

to jeopardize this and you'd be forced to terminate him."

Dominic had the same fear. Angelina was the only authority the boy had known for many years and he was used to answering to no one, not even the law.

But that had changed when Dominic had talked to Renni. Dominic had made it very clear that if Renni wanted to stay out of jail, he had to support himself and not involve his sister in any more nefarious activities.

And so far…for two weeks, Renni had kept his word. And for Angelina's sake, Dominic hoped that would continue. He'd learned that Angelina had a very soft heart where her brother was concerned.

And a jealous part of him wanted her to care and worry over him the same way. And he knew she'd never be able to do that if he sent her brother to jail.

He had found that he liked spending as much time with Angelina as he could. Living in two separate places had been difficult and he'd moved as quickly as he could to get them under one roof. This place was very upscale and sophisticated, befitting a man of his stature. But to be honest he didn't care about that. He had just wanted to give something to Angelina that she couldn't have gotten for herself.

"I understand about brothers," Dominic said. He'd tried to keep things light between the two of them, but he was a bit on edge waiting to see if Ian could find another connection to Barty Eastburn. Barty hadn't shown up for the meeting with Angelina, so that meant they had to find evidence against Eastburn another way. They suspected Barty knew Angelina had given herself up to Dominic.

"What are you thinking?"

"About work."

"What about it? I finished sending the final plans for the new Vallerio motor to the design group today. I know everyone is ecstatic over the fact that you are now officially going forward with the revamped Vallerio Roadster."

"Yes, they are," he said. The one nice thing about having an affair with Angelina was the freedom to talk about his work with her. But there were times, like now, when he wanted to remind her that the information she was discussing was still meant to be kept under wraps. "You know that this needs to be kept quiet."

"I do. I wouldn't have said anything except that I thought it might be on your mind," she said. Before they'd become lovers Angelina had been spunky and always standing up to him, but now she backed down quickly if she thought she'd upset him.

"Why do you always do that?"

"What?"

"Back down and apologize for everything."

"I'm just trying to be nice."

"Nice?"

She nodded.

"Don't be. You should know me well enough to realize that I don't like yes men."

She tipped her head to the side and gave him a very shrewd look. "But you do like accommodating women."

"True enough, but I know how to get you to be more biddable."

"You do?"

"Indeed. Come here and I'll prove it."

She shook her head. "You come here."

"That's not what I asked. You want to be nice to me, don't you, Angelina?"

She hesitated and he had no idea what she was thinking but the emotions that moved across her face were easy to identify. Fear, hope and something that looked a lot like caring.

"I'm always nice to you. I got your breakfast without complaining," she said.

This morning he'd had an important meeting with both of his brothers and there simply hadn't been time to order in as they usually did, so he'd had Angelina run out and get them breakfast. Normally he wouldn't have asked her to do that kind of thing since she was his assistant, but he had to admit he'd wanted her out of the office while Antonio brought them up to date on what was going on with Vallerio Inc.

"I made that up to you," he said. He'd taken her to lunch in the piazza and bought her the pretty gold charm bracelet, which now graced her slim wrist.

"Yes, you did. Did I thank you properly for that?"

He nodded. "Are you going to come over here or not?"

"That depends."

"On what?"

"If you are going to use your body to distract me."

"You don't like that?" he asked.

"I love it," she said. "I had no idea how sexy you could be, Dominic."

He arched one eyebrow at her. "You didn't find me attractive before our affair started?"

"I did. I just didn't allow myself to think about you in...carnal terms."

He laughed. There was something about Angelina when she let her hair down that made him relax and forget that he always had to be on his guard. Always keep his eye on the prize as his grandfather had told him on his deathbed.

"You mean you didn't lust after me?"

She shook her head. "I had plenty of lust, I just didn't think that you'd ever want me. Or that I'd ever be here with you like this."

"And now that you are?"

"I'm afraid that it's going to end all too soon."

Eight

Angelina had been surprised by Dominic's invitation for her to attend Moretti Motors' reception debuting their new roadster. But she'd happily agreed.

The entire Vallerio Inc. board had flown in from France to attend. Angelina suspected they were also here to celebrate Nathalie's engagement to Antonio.

She liked Nathalie a lot. They had become friends over the long weeks that Nathalie had spent in Milan negotiating with Antonio.

She knew that both Moretti Motors and

Vallerio Inc. were in talks to release the coupe version of the car next year as well.

"*Bonjour,* Nathalie. Congratulations on your engagement," Angelina said, moving to where the woman stood near a tall cocktail table.

"Thank you," Nathalie said. "I still can't believe I'm going to marry a Moretti. My grandfather is either laughing with delight that I caught a Moretti or spinning in anger that once again a Moretti caught a Vallerio."

"Wasn't your grandfather good friends with Lorenzo Moretti?"

"Yes, until Lorenzo broke my *tante* Anna's heart. Very tragic…I'm making light but it was sad. It seems like Lorenzo Moretti was doomed when it came to women."

"Cursed," Dominic said, coming up behind the two women. He held a champagne flute in each hand. He looked dashing in his tux as he handed one of the glasses to her.

She took it, lifting it toward him in a salute. "To Moretti Motors continued success."

He clinked his glass to hers and they both took a drink.

"You don't believe there is still a curse, do

you?" Nathalie asked. "I thought that Marco and Virginia broke it when Enzo was born."

Angelina had only heard rumors about the Moretti curse. The gossip was that the Moretti men could either be lucky in business or lucky in love, but never in both. Lorenzo Moretti, the founder of Moretti Motors, had been lucky in business turning the small company he started into one of the world's top luxury automakers. His son Giovanni had been lucky in business until he'd fallen in love with Philomena at which time Moretti Motors started to fail. Dominic, Antonio and Marco had decided that they would be the generation to be lucky in business again.

"How could the curse be broken?" Angelina asked.

"Virginia is the granddaughter of Cassia Festa, the woman who cursed my *nono*. And she had access to the original language that Cassia had used to cast that curse. She read over the words and figured out the meaning behind the curse and then deemed that if Moretti and Festa blood were mingled the curse would be broken," Dominic said.

"So now there's no more curse?" Angelina asked.

Dominic shrugged. "Who worries about curses when they are as successful as I am?"

She smiled because she knew he'd meant her to. But she wasn't feeling it. Instead she was worried that Dominic didn't seem to care that his family's curse meant that the men were destined for either fortune or love.

Though to be fair, Marco and Virginia seemed very happy. Marco's fortune hadn't changed and he was still winning F1 races. Antonio and Nathalie hadn't been together that long, but Angelina didn't see any signs that either Moretti Motors or Vallerio Inc. was going to face financial hardship.

"Dominic, you are never going to convince a woman to stick around with that kind of attitude," Nathalie said.

"I have other attributes you might not be as aware of."

"She better not be," Antonio said, coming up behind his fiancée. He hugged her close and dropped a quick kiss on Nathalie's lips.

"*Buona sera,* Angelina."

"Good evening, Antonio." She wasn't too certain what Antonio thought of her. She knew that all of the Moretti brothers were aware she had been spying on the company and that made her feel as though she didn't deserve the happiness she had found with Dominic. Maybe she was starting her own bad luck.

"I don't mean to hurry everyone away, but we need to mingle. Marco and the rest of Team Moretti should be arriving any minute and many of the guests will want to talk to him and Keke," Dominic said.

Keke had been a Team Moretti F1 driver who had been injured in a car accident; actually he'd almost died. And Angelina remembered how upset the Morettis had been about it. They treated everyone who worked for the company like family.

Like a real family, she realized. Not at all the way she and Renni had been because it was just the two of them. But a big extended group of people that she could rely on. It was a different kind of feeling and she liked it.

"Angelina?"

"Hmm?"

"I need you to entertain the press group," Dominic said.

"Certainly. What do you want me to do?" Angelina asked.

"Just the tour of the factory like we discussed earlier," Dominic said.

Everyone at the reception would be taken on a factory tour in small groups. Angelina was happy to be included as one of the Moretti Motors representatives. She knew it wasn't so much due to her being Dominic's mistress but more because he was starting to trust her again.

Angelina was tired a bit after the long day at work. Dominic was out of town for an F1 race all of the Morettis traditionally attended. She felt very much his mistress when he left her behind in Milan, which made her feel foolish besides.

Dominic hadn't promised her any more than he'd given her. He treated her well. She unlocked the door to the apartment he'd insisted they live in. The welcoming scent of orange blossoms greeted her as she put her keys on the hall table and walked into the living area. There was a crisp breeze blowing in from the balcony.

"*Sì,* Angelina. I'm sorry I didn't call. I got an earlier flight back."

"I'm so glad," she said. "I missed you."

"Good."

"You can be very arrogant at times."

"You're right I can. Did you miss me in bed?"

he asked, crossing the room and taking her in his arms.

"Yes," she said. She had missed his arms around her during the night and the comfort she took from knowing he was there next to her.

"Me, too. I didn't expect to miss you," he said, his confession coming quietly from him.

"Me either," she said. He led the way to the couch and sat down, pulling her down on his lap.

He kissed her passionately and she pulled back. "Can we pause for a bit?"

"Why?" he asked.

"It's…it's been a long day," she said, holding herself stiffly. "I think I'd be happy to have your arms around me."

She knew she was being needy, and a part of her wanted to push hard to see exactly what she meant to Dominic. If he pushed her away, then she would simply try to stop caring for him. Try to keep herself from falling for him.

"I'd love to hold you. Go change into something comfortable and get into bed. Have you eaten?"

She shook her head. "But I'm not hungry."

"I will join you in a minute."

Angelina left Dominic in the living room to go

and get changed. She took her time washing her face, and tried not to read too much into Dominic's actions. He was a kind man—she shouldn't be surprised that he'd take care of her when she didn't feel well.

But what did surprise her was that he'd do something so unselfish for her. There was nothing for him in his comforting her. Nothing at all. And she knew she hadn't been able to get any further information from Barty or ESP Motors, but tonight it didn't seem to matter.

Tonight it felt to her as if Dominic cared about her simply because she was his woman.

She changed into the silk pajamas she kept on a hook on the back of the bathroom door and came out to find the covers turned back on the bed. Dominic had stripped down to his boxers and a T-shirt.

He held his hand out to her and she went to him. She climbed into the bed on his side and then slid over. He got in after her and pulled covers over her before drawing her close to his side. She rested her head on his shoulder and closed her eyes, relaxing for the first time…since her mother had died. No one had held her like this since her parents had died.

She sniffed, trying not to cry thinking about the hugs that she missed.

"What's the matter?"

"Nothing. I was just thinking of the past," she said.

"What about it?"

"My parents. I didn't realize until this moment how much I missed the simple things they did for me."

He hugged her closer, dropping a kiss on the top of her head.

"You lost someone to share your life with," he said.

"Yes, and my dreams."

"What are you dreams, *cara mia?* Share them with me," he said, stroking his hand down her back.

She shifted in his arms until his hand was rubbing right where she ached. "I don't know what my dreams are anymore. I think I've always wanted to live in the countryside, have a family of my own."

"Would you stay at home with the children?" he asked her.

"Yes, I'd like that very much. I know that might not be possible, but I'd be willing to sacrifice material things if I had to. What about you?" she asked, meeting his dark gaze with her own.

"I think I'd like my wife to stay home with the kids. My mother was there for my brothers and me after school. She had her own life during the day, but we knew she was there…I think that's very important for children."

"I agree," she said. She tipped her head down and closed her eyes. She didn't like to think of Dominic married and having children, because she had started thinking of him as her man and now she knew that he probably wouldn't be.

Dominic fielded questions from the international television media as he led his group through the factory. So far all of the comments and questions he'd received had been very promising. They'd had a request from BBC's Top Gear to test out the Vallerio Roadster, which pleased him.

It was the kind of press they could use. Nathalie was charming a group of investors from France and Antonio was scowling each time Nathalie laughed at something one of the men in her group said. Dominic thought it was funny that his brother, who had never been tempted by any one woman, was now so tied in knots over his fiery redhead.

He escorted the last group through the factory and noticed that Renaldo De Luca was still in the work area. He should have been at the reception and not back here. Renaldo smiled at Dominic when he saw him and waved, then gestured to the pretty girl with him.

Dominic took out his mobile phone and sent a quick text message to Angelina asking her to get her brother and his date out of the factory. This wasn't the place for romance—especially tonight.

She immediately responded that she would take care of it. Dominic wondered if she would ever really be able to get her wayward brother under control. He doubted it, because for some reason Renni cared only about himself.

"That concludes our tour. Tomorrow starting at ten a.m. we will be offering test rides in the Roadster out at our track. You can sign up for a ride at the desk near the far side of the room. I hope you enjoy the rest of the evening."

As his group dissipated, Dominic saw Ian moving toward him. The other man looked as though there was something important on his mind.

"Got a minute?" Ian asked as soon as he was close enough to be heard.

"Yes. Here or in my office?"

"Office would be better," Ian said.

"Should I get Marco and Antonio?"

"I think you might want to hear this first."

Dominic didn't like the feeling generating in the pit of his stomach. He glanced around the reception area and didn't see Angelina. "Give me a minute."

"No problem."

Dominic left the reception area to go back to the factory. The last of the tours had moved through and the factory was eerily empty.

He heard the sound of voices and wasn't surprised to find that Renaldo and Angelina were the source. "I told you not to mess this up."

"I didn't, Ange. I just wanted to be alone with Penni. I'm sorry, it was stupid to come in here."

"It was stupid to bring her in here. Everything in this room is still under wraps."

"I said I'm sorry. What more do you want?"

She shook her head. "I want you to be a man, Renni."

"I have been since Dad died."

She shook her head. "No, you haven't. You say that, but not one time have you stepped up and taken care of something for me. Or taken care of me, your only sister—that's what men do."

"I can't live up to the standards set by your precious Dominic."

She shook her head. "I'm not asking you to. I want you to be your own man. To think before you act and for once handle something on your own."

"I am trying, Ange. I really am. I will find Dominic and tell him I'm sorry about being in here."

She took a deep breath. "Okay, you do that. But he might not want you to keep working for him."

"Then that's the price I'll have to pay."

Dominic heard something in Renaldo's voice he'd never heard before, and it sounded like responsibility. He didn't expect anyone to be perfect, and Renaldo's actions tonight were harmless.

"There you two are," he said, stepping out of the shadows.

Both of them turned to face him. Angelina took a step forward, but Renaldo stopped her with his hand on her shoulder.

"I'm sorry, Signore Moretti. I didn't think tonight when I brought Penni back here."

"No, you didn't think. Apology accepted."

"It won't happen again," Renaldo said.

"I know it won't," Dominic said. He believed

that Renaldo was starting to grow up. Maybe it had been his sister's tears or the fact that she'd almost had to go to jail for him, but something had woken Renaldo De Luca up.

"Go and enjoy the rest of the party," Dominic said.

"Yes, sir."

Renaldo left and Angelina still didn't look at him. She was beautiful tonight in her formal dress. It was black—as most of her clothing was—and formfitting. Her shoulders and neck were bare and as she kept staring at the floor he couldn't help but notice how vulnerable she looked.

"What are you thinking?" he asked.

She lifted her head and he saw the glitter of tears in her eyes. "Thank you for going easy on him."

"No need to thank me. I know that mistakes happen, and owning up to them like he did shows me the kind of man he's becoming."

She nodded. "I…I've been so worried about him."

"Why?"

"Because I haven't let him fight any of his own battles. He was devastated when Mom and Dad died…you can't imagine what it was like that first year."

Dominic crossed the space between them and drew her into his arms. He wished he'd been there for Angelina then. Wait a minute. What was he thinking? If he'd been there for her, he probably wouldn't have any of the things that he called his own today.

Angelina was a distraction to him, and though he'd never lose his business focus, if he'd met her before he'd gotten involved in the day-to-day running of Moretti Motors, he'd easily have been content to let himself fall in love with her. Damn, was that what he was doing?

That couldn't be right. And if it was, it meant she was too much of a distraction. If he let her take over any part of his life, Moretti Motors would fall back into the hands of outsiders. One thing that Dominic promised himself he'd never let happen.

Would he, though? He'd had a chance at love and had blown it. In college he'd fallen hard for a pretty American named Kate, and they'd become engaged after one semester. Dominic had thought that Kate was his world and expected her to feel the same about him. But she'd returned home to Texas for the summer while he worked in Moretti Motors as a management trainee. When it was time to return to school, Kate had called him and said she wasn't coming back. She missed the States and her home there too much. Dominic had thought about leaving Moretti Motors and going to her, but she'd discouraged him from doing so.

Why then did his heart feel as though Angelina was the missing piece?

After that night at the reception Angelina noticed a change in their relationship. Dominic stopped treating her like a mistress and more like a girlfriend. More like a woman he was going to continue seeing. But it had been almost six months now and she lived on pins and needles, so afraid that Dominic would stick to the letter of the agreement they'd signed.

"Want to go out for a drink after work?" Marta asked while they were at lunch.

"I can't."

"Do you have a date?" Marta asked.

"Yes," she said.

"Well, me, too, but not until later," Marta said.

"Still computer dating?"

"Yes. I know my Mr. Right is out there."

"What do you mean your Mr. Right?"

"The one guy meant for me. Do you believe in that?" Marta asked.

Angelina shrugged. "I've never really thought about it. I've never dated a lot. But, with Renni relying on me I couldn't."

"But that's not a problem anymore, is it? I meant to tell you your brother is one hot guy. I'd think about asking him out, except I know all his dirt from you."

Angelina laughed at her friend. Marta didn't know the half of what Renni had done and she never would. As far as Angelina was concerned, Renni's troubles in London were a different lifetime. They'd both moved on and were in a much better place now.

"So who's your date with, some hottie?"

"Yes, he's a hottie."

"And a mystery man? Is it someone from work?" Marta asked, glancing around the cafeteria. She leaned across the table. "I won't tell a soul."

For the first time Angelina was tempted to tell Marta her personal business. But she couldn't break a lifetime of habits and she was used to keeping her own counsel. She'd never been a woman to share secrets with girlfiends even when she'd been younger.

"Yes, someone from work. But I don't want to talk too much about it."

"Is the relationship serious?" Marta asked.

Angelina glanced down at the salad she was eating. She had no idea. She looked at the charm bracelet Dominic had bought her back at the beginning of their relationship. It was laden with charms he'd given her over the last six months. He'd given her other jewelry, more expensive pieces that she suspected he'd given to his other mistresses as well. But this was the one piece that meant the most to her.

"Oh, no," Marta said.

"What?"

"Your silence tells me two things."

Angelina looked up, waiting to hear what her friend was going to say.

"Either he's married—"

"He's not. I wouldn't get involved with a man who was married."

Marta shrugged. "I wouldn't judge you. Falling in love is something that happens when you least expect it. It's the Mr. Right thing. Sometimes he's already in a doomed relationship."

She didn't know that she agreed with Marta, but she did know that Dominic was hers. She shook her head. Was that really it? Of course it was. She loved Dominic. She wouldn't have agreed to be the mistress of any other man.

Only Dominic Moretti because he was the only man who made her feel alive and…complete.

"What else do you think my silence means?" Angelina asked.

"That you care more for him than he does for you," Marta said.

Angelina could only stare at her American friend.

"Why are you looking at me like that?" Marta asked.

"Because you saw something that I was afraid to admit."

"It's not because I'm wise or anything—it's just that I've been there before. Why do you think I came to Milan?"

"Why?"

"To escape. I was tired of seeing him every day and not being able to be with him. Even after I moved out of the neighborhood where we'd once lived and changed jobs…he haunted me."

Angelina reached across the table and took Marta's hand, squeezing it to offer some comfort for the pain she saw in the other woman's eyes. But then Marta shook her head. "But that is all in the past. He wasn't my Mr. Right, and moving on was the only sensible thing to do. So what about your guy?"

Angelina wasn't sure she bought in to Marta's little pep talk, but it was clear that her friend was trying to cheer her up. "What about him?"

"Is he a lost cause or do you think he will fall for you?"

Angelina thought about the way Dominic held her in bed every night. How he'd pull her close to his side and hold her until he drifted off. That felt like more than lust.

And he really did take care of her—and not just sexually or even financially. He was willing to hold her when PMS made her weepy or to listen to her talk about her dreams of living in a little house in the countryside instead of in the city center of Milan.

"There are times when I think… Well, yes, he is my man."

Marta glanced at her watch. "I have to get back to work. I hope for your sake that he is the man you think he is."

Angelina shared that hope. In fact, she was risking her heart on that hope. And tonight she was going to take a big risk and ask Dominic to continue their relationship after their agreement ended.

Nine

"Where is Angelina?" Antonio asked as he walked into Dominic's office.

Dominic glanced at his TAG Heuer watch before responding. "At home getting ready for our date tonight."

"Date? Are you sure you know what you are doing with her? I didn't say anything when you completely ignored the fact that she was stealing from us and moved in with her, but are you really using your best judgment?"

"I am not doing anything that would put the company in jeopardy. You and I both know it wasn't her choice to pass that information to ESP. They are the ones we want to catch, not her. Trust me."

"I do. If it wasn't for you I don't know where we would all be today. It was your vision to bring Moretti Motors back to the glory it experienced during *Nono*'s heyday."

"What's your point?"

"I don't want to see you get hurt with this woman, Dom. You know she's betrayed us once."

"I do know that. But she was doing it to protect her brother."

"What makes you so certain she won't have to protect him again?"

"Because Renaldo is now owning up to his life," Dominic said. He didn't want to discuss his personal life with his brother. Antonio had done his own thing, gone against Dominic's wishes and fallen in love with Nathalie Vallerio. A move that had almost cost them the rights to the Vallerio name.

"You weren't exactly thinking with your brain when you fell for Nathalie."

"My point exactly. That's why I'm talking to you now."

"What do you want from me?" Dominic asked.

"Just be careful, Dom. We don't know if Angelina is completely trustworthy."

"There hasn't been a leak in over six months and Ian has been working closely to make sure that Barty Eastburn hasn't recruited anyone else from our company."

"Fair enough. I wanted to talk to you about the press release we are sending out for tomorrow. I know that you approved it, but we need to change the wording on the Vallerio Incorporated section."

They discussed what needed to be changed. Press releases were normally handled through the publicity department. But because this was the big launch of a new type of engine that Moretti Motors had won exclusive rights to use from Vallerio Inc. both Dominic and Antonio had decided to vet the release.

By the time the meeting ended he realized he was going to be late for his date with Angelina. Antonio was almost out the door when Dominic stopped him.

"Do you think the curse is broken?" he asked.

"Yes. The way I feel about Nathalie has shown me that I can have it all. It didn't make me not want Moretti Motors to succeed anymore. In fact, because of our joint ventures with Vallerio Incorporated, I'm even more determined to see that we continue to grow our business."

Dominic nodded. "I wondered if *Nono* cursed himself because he gave up the woman he loved."

"He might have. For him it was Moretti Motors or nothing. He would never have been able to make a relationship work while running this company," Antonio said.

"I agree. It was in *Nono*'s nature never to put anyone before Moretti Motors," Dominic said. "Though Dad is the opposite."

"Yes, he is. Are you serious about Angelina?"

Dominic shrugged. "I think I am. We had an agreement…but I'm thinking of asking her to make it permanent."

"Permanent as in marriage?"

"Not marriage but a long-term affair." Dominic had thought of little else for the last two months. He couldn't say for sure what it was that had made him start thinking of a future with Angelina, but something had. He only knew that when he'd started thinking about living without her, he'd felt hollow inside.

"Am I being a fool?" he asked his brother.

"Love is a tricky thing…"

"I'm not in love. She just makes my life comfortable away from work. She gives me companionship."

Antonio watched him with those shrewd eyes of his. "I don't know what to tell you, bro. Nathalie added something to my life that I didn't realize was missing until she was there. Is that how you feel about Angelina?"

Dominic shrugged. He shouldn't have started this conversation. Whenever he discussed anything but Moretti Motors he felt as though he was out of his league. He loved his family, but women had always been a bit of a mystery to him. "I don't know. I only feel that I want her by my side."

"Then go for it. You know we focus a lot on being *Nono*'s grandsons, but we are also Papa's sons. And that man is a romantic. A man who knows that passion for a woman is the greatest joy one can find."

"*Grazie,* Tony."

Antonio wraggled his eyebrows at Dominic, a goofy thing his brother had done since they were boys. "Don't mention it. Everyone knows I'm the smooth lover in the family."

Dominic punched his brother in the shoulder. "Everyone knows you are the goof-off."

"Very true," Antonio said. "It's because I'm happy. Everything with Moretti Motors is going as we planned. I have a woman I love in my life… Who could ask for anything more?"

Dominic walked out of the building with his brother, realizing for the first time that he wanted what Antonio and Marco had found with their women. And that life was finally within his grasp with Angelina.

Angelina loved driving with Dominic. It was easy to tell he was the grandson of a legendary F1 driver and the brother of another. His skills behind the wheel were superb and he put her at ease as he wove through the evening traffic in Milan as they headed out of the city.

"Where are we going?" she asked as he fiddled with the radio, putting on a CD of her favorite artist. Angelina rested her head against the back of the seat trying not to read more into this moment, this night, than she should.

Because of the nature of their relationship they'd spent a lot of time going to private places for dates or just staying at the penthouse apartment.

"Lake Como. Is that okay?"

She nodded. "I love it there. When I was a child we used to go for holidays."

"My family had a house there, as well. When we were boys we spent a lot of time on the lake."

"What was it like growing up with two brothers?" Angelina asked. "I love Renni, but I would have liked a sister."

"My brothers are the best friends that I have. From the time I was very young I was aware of our family's legacy from Grandfather—"

"The curse?"

"*Sì.* And as I got older I realized that I didn't want to take a chance on letting Moretti Motors slip further away from our family. It was important to me that Tony and Marco both realized what a gift our grandfather had left us," Dominic said.

"I can see that. You did a good job of rebuilding the company. That was one of the things that drew me to Moretti Motors when I was job hunting."

"It was?"

"*Sì.* I wanted to work for a company with corporate integrity and wasn't just about money. Your organization has a sense of pride in everything that Moretti Motors does be it the retail luxury car market or your F1 team."

Dominic glanced over at her. "Reputation is really all we have that we can call our own. Fortunes can be won or lost."

She reached over and squeezed his thigh.

"What was that for?"

She rubbed her finger in a little circle pattern on his leg. "I'm sorry I almost ruined your reputation by stealing information."

He put his hand over hers. His big fingers engulfed her smaller ones and he lifted her hand to his lips, brushing them against the center of her palm.

"We are past that now, aren't we?" Dominic asked.

"I still feel...shame, I guess, about what I did." It was more than that. She hated that the reason he'd noticed her as a woman and not just his assistant was tied to that act of betrayal. And no matter how much she tried to tell herself that it didn't matter, a big part of her knew it did.

"You have to let it go. I did."

"Did you?" she asked, trying not to be distracted by the movement of his thigh muscles under her hand.

"Yes. Though it was hard for me because your actions felt like disloyalty. And I'm also a bit jealous that you would go to another man," he said. There was a bit of vehemence in his voice that suggested he might not be as forgiving as he'd said.

"I never had a loyalty to anyone but you and to my family."

"And that is why I am letting it go. That and the fact that we can never have any kind of relationship if I didn't."

She caught her breath. "Relationship? Do you mean something beyond the six months we agreed to?"

He glanced over at her. "I do mean that, Angelina, but we will talk when we get to my villa."

She felt a flutter in the pit of her stomach, and for the first time since her parents died that scared, lonely part of her relaxed. The feelings she had for Dominic were strong, and knowing that he wanted to continue the relationship with her made her realize that Marta had a point to something she'd said earlier.

There was a Mr. Right for each woman, and Dominic was hers.

"Tell me about your holidays at Lake Como," he said.

"My grandparents brought us one summer. Only that once. Renni and I were eight and ten and *Nono* rented a boat and we spent all day on the lake. I pretended I was a princess and Renni was a pirate."

He glanced over at her and smiled. "Sounds like it was fun."

It had been. "It was. I haven't thought of that time in years."

"That's natural. You're not someone who looks back all the time."

"True. Life is lived in the now, isn't it? I learned that from working with you. When someone makes a mistake you don't brush it aside, but you learn from it as you move on. I had never seen anyone do that before."

"Given the nature of my family, it's either learn and move on or wither and die talking about the glory days. And talking isn't productive."

"Isn't it?"

"Not unless there's a purpose to it."

He continued talking to her about his life philosophy, and she listened, soaking up the sound of his voice and the feel of his leg under her hand. She liked the connection she felt to Dominic and realized that no matter what happened later in their relationship, he'd given her something that no one else had.

He'd given her the belief in herself that she was more than worthy of being his woman.

Their drive continued. The moon was full and the late-summer sky bright. She couldn't wait for the start of autumn.

"Tell me about your holidays on Lake Como," she said.

He thought back to those long days when he'd been a young boy. "When I was eight or so, I didn't realize we were the poor relations. My grandfather had let us move into his compound in Milan since my mother worked nearby, and he had servants to help during the day with raising us."

"What changed?" she asked.

He was a man who'd built his life on pride. He admitted that and knew that how the world perceived him was important to him. "It was that summer. Tony and I used to gang up on Marco… What can I say—he was an annoying little brother."

"Aren't they all?" she said with a hint of laughter in her voice.

"Indeed. Well, we dared Marco to jump out of the tree house my father had built for us. And his friend Gui was visiting with us, as well. So Marco and Gui go up in the tree house and jump from the platform. It was about three meters high, and when Marco landed he twisted his knee and broke his leg. Gui was right alongside him and only twisted his ankle."

"You must have been upset that he got hurt, but how did that change your perception of money?"

"Gui's family was very angry and threatened to sue my parents for negligence. It was a bigger deal than we imagined, and my grandfather pulled us aside and told us to stop being so...ridiculous—that's the term he used. He said that one generation of Morettis had squandered their money and not to let our generation continue the pattern."

Angelina reached over and squeezed his thigh. "You were just a boy."

"I was old enough to know that what I'd done was wrong. My mother was upset because we might have to sell the Lake Como house. It had been a wedding gift from her parents."

"I am so sorry. So one act of brotherly teasing changed the direction of your life?" she asked.

He shrugged. "I probably would still be who I am today, but that incident made me stop being so irresponsible."

His cell phone rang and he let go of her hand to answer it.

"It's Stark. We need to talk."

"Tonight, Ian?"

"Yes. I have some important information on the investigation… Dammit. A cop just pulled me over," Ian said.

"What for?"

"Driving and talking on my cell phone. It's illegal in London."

"Call me back," Dominic said.

"I will."

Dominic disconnected the call.

"What did Ian want on the phone?" she asked.

"He's had a break in the ESP Motors investigation," he answered at length.

"Good," she said. "I'll be very happy when that entire mess is behind us."

"Will you?"

"Yes, I regret ever doing anything to make you feel like you were betrayed."

He nodded. Her words cemented in his mind that asking her to continue their relationship was the right choice. She had made a mistake and she had changed. He'd seen the evidence himself over the past six months. And he knew he didn't want to go back to the way life had been before he'd blackmailed her into his bed.

Ten

Dominic had arranged to have dinner set up on his Lake Como villa's veranda. His parents' house was a few miles up the road and Antonio and Marco both had their own places here as well. Lake Como was where they all called home.

Lake Como was a beautiful area frequented by the jet-set crowd. Millionaire businessmen, heads of state and Hollywood celebrities all owned property here, but that wasn't what had drawn him here. It had been the tranquility of the area and the fact that this was the one place where his parents had always managed to keep a home.

Because his mom's family had gifted the property to them, it had been a matter of pride that his father had never sold that house.

When his father had lost the chairmanship of Moretti Motors, their immediate family fortune had changed. They'd been forced to sell their house in San Giuliano Milanese and had to live with distant relatives until his mother started making decent money as a teacher at a local university.

"I love this place," Angelina said as she walked out of the living room area onto the veranda.

"Me, too. I'm sorry we haven't had time to come out here before this."

"It's been a busy summer," she said. "Next year will be calmer once we get the Vallerio launched."

"Indeed it will be," he said. Next summer he'd spend more time at the lake with Angelina and his brothers. Marco was thinking of retiring from F1 racing and he would take over managing Team Moretti when he did. That would give Dominic one less responsibility at work. And he could spend the extra time with Angelina.

"I have something important to talk to you about."

"You mentioned our relationship in the car."

He walked to the balustrade's railing and leaned against it. Angelina looked exquisite in the mood lighting. Her hair curled around her pretty face and her dress clung to her curves. Her nipples were visible under the bodice of her dress and he still had her panties in his jacket pocket.

She was completely bare under that dress and he wondered if conversation was really what he wanted right now. He knew it wasn't. He was still aroused from her hand on him in the car and he wanted to say the hell with talking and just lift her skirt and take her.

But lust wasn't the problem between them. Communication was. And he needed things to be settled between them. He needed to know that she was his for the foreseeable future. He needed…her.

"You're staring at me." Angelina's voice interrupted his thoughts.

"Am I?"

"Yes, you are. What are you thinking, Dominic?"

"I'm wondering what you feel for me," he said.

She took a deep breath and walked toward him, her hips swaying gently with each step. She stopped when she was at his side and leaned forward, resting her arms against the banister as she stared at the horizon. "Why do you want to know?"

He turned to face the same direction as she was and moved to stand behind her. He placed his hands on either side of her body and leaned over her.

"Because I care for you, Angelina," he said, speaking directly into her ear. "And I have no idea if your feelings for me have changed."

She turned her head to the side, brushing her lips over his jaw. "I care for you so much, Dominic."

"How much?"

She shook her head, her silky curls rubbing against his face. "I'm afraid to tell you."

"Why?"

She took a deep breath and then looked at him. Met his gaze head-on and he felt the impact of her emotions. "Because if you don't feel the same way about me, I'm going to feel very vulnerable."

"I will protect you, Angelina. Even your feelings. Haven't I done that very thing from the beginning?"

"Yes, you have," she said. "Even when it

wasn't in your best interest to look out for me, you did. Why did you do that?"

He definitely wasn't going to tell her that he'd done it for one reason and one reason alone. He could only guess that he'd started loving her a long time ago.

He wrapped his arm around her middle and pulled her back against the curve of his body. Damn, she was a weakness he hadn't anticipated. A weakness that he knew could be his downfall.

Women and Moretti Motors didn't mix. Yet he didn't want to let her go. "Tell me how you feel," he said. He put his mouth to her neck and nibbled at her skin.

She shifted in his arms, turning to face him. She went up on tiptoe and kissed him deeply. Her tongue slid over his and he was struck again by how right she felt in his arms.

He took control of the kiss and she twisted against him sinuously. He lifted her, setting her on the banister.

He pulled up her skirt and then lowered his zipper. He didn't take the time for a condom, needing to be inside her. He kept his erection poised to enter her body and felt the damp wetness of her welcome him.

"Tell me," he said, swiveling his hips to tease her.

She put her hands on his shoulders and leaned down to bite his earlobe.

"*Ti amo,* Dominic Moretti. I love you."

"Very good," he said, entering her with one long stroke. He took them both quickly to the pinnacle of release and they climaxed together. Dominic had the answers he hadn't realized he'd been seeking and it surprised him that they were right here in his arms. That this one woman was the thing that he hadn't been able to find on his own or in his success at Moretti Motors.

Angelina sat across the table from Dominic enjoying the dinner his staff had prepared and trying very hard not to dwell on the fact that she'd told him she loved him and he hadn't said it back.

She felt incredibly exposed at this moment. She'd never been more nervous of the outcome of a meal. What if she was like poor Marta, haunted by Dominic until she had to leave not only Milan but Italy? What if…

"Do you like the veal?" Dominic asked.

He was relaxed and in a very good mood. Something she'd noticed early on in their relationship that sex did for him. It relaxed her, too, and normally she loved seeing his face so calm and his easy smile.

But a knot had formed in the pit of her stomach and she knew that until he told her how he felt, it wasn't going to go away.

"It's very good," she said, putting her fork down and reaching across the table for her wineglass. She took one deep swallow and then another.

"Are you okay?"

"I need to ask you something," she said.

"Okay." He, too, put his fork his down and leaned back in his chair.

A gentle breeze blew up from the lake, stirring the hair at the back of her neck. She closed her eyes for a minute and let go of the sense of panic she felt. What did it matter how Dominic felt toward her? Her love for him wasn't going to change.

But she knew that if he didn't love her she'd end up being the one to carry the burden of their relationship and it would never be balanced. That was something she'd learned the hard way with Renni. And it was only Dominic who'd shown her that she couldn't always be the one to rescue Renni; he had to do it for himself.

"Angelina?"

"I'm sorry. It's just this is harder to say than I thought it would be."

"What is this about? Have you been in contact with Eastburn again?"

She shook her head. "No. Why would you think that? I told you that I wasn't going to steal anything else from Moretti Motors."

Dominic took a swallow of his wine. "You are clearly nervous and can't find the words to tell me whatever is on your mind."

She twisted her fingers together, tried not to let his accusation stand between them, but it did. And before she could ask him about his feelings, they needed to clear the air about their past.

"You said you'd forgiven me for what I'd done, but I think I need more than that."

"Okay, what do you want from me?"

"I guess some kind of acknowledgment that you know I'm not a thief. I had never taken anything before this incident and I haven't done anything since. If you can't see beyond the circumstances that caused me to make that bad decision, then I guess we don't have anything else to say to each other."

"I can. I understand that your brother is your weakness. He's the only man you care about."

She shook her head. "He's not the only man I care about, Dominic. I also care deeply for you. I told you I loved you. Did you think I was lying?"

"I never thought you lied about your feelings. I just don't know anything else that would make you this nervous. The last time you were this way, I had a meeting with Ian and learned that you were the spy. Can you understand my reaction?"

"Yes. I'm sorry about my part in this. I was just trying to find the words to ask you about your feelings for me. But now I feel stupid that I made it into something else."

Angelina felt small and more exposed than ever.

"Angelina, *mia bella,* don't apologize. I jumped to conclusions."

"Why?" she asked.

"I am nervous, too," he said.

She laughed.

"That wasn't very nice."

"I'm sorry but Dominic Moretti is never nervous. You are the one who strikes fear into your competitors."

He reached over and stroked her face, something she noticed he liked to do. "That is very true. But you aren't a competitor, Angelina."

"No, I'm not. I'm just the woman who loves you," she said. Having confessed her feelings, she was finding that she liked expressing them.

"I like hearing you say that," he said.

"I like saying it. I can't believe how my life has changed," she said. "To go from the constant fear that I'd be arrested to having you…it's more than I dreamed possible. Sometimes I almost don't believe that this is real. That you are my lover and that the life we've been living is mine."

"I don't want you to fear anymore. I brought you here tonight to ask you to keep living with me," he said.

"Another arrangement?"

He shook his head. "I think we are beyond that. I don't want you to be my mistress any longer. I don't want to hide our relationship from our friends."

"Oh, Dominic," she said. "That is what I want, too."

"Good," he said. "Then it's settled."

"Not yet."

"What else is there?"

"I want to know how you feel about me," she said.

"I care about you very much, Angelina."

"Just care?"

"No, it's more than—"

"Signore Moretti," his butler, Gennaro, interrupted from the doorway. "I'm sorry to bother you but you have an urgent call from Signore Stark."

"I'll be right back," Dominic said to Angelina, and she nodded. She could wait to hear him say he loved her. It would be a bit of icing on a night that was already more perfect than she could have imagined.

Dominic stalked into his library and answered the landline that Ian had called on. "Moretti here."

"Why haven't you been answering your mobile?"

"I turned it off to enjoy the evening with Angelina. I didn't want anything to interrupt us. Which you are doing right now. What do you have for me?"

"Big news. ESP Motors is having a press conference tomorrow to announce a new engine design that they are putting into production on all of their cars."

"You called me for this? We leaked the wrong plans, you know that. All that Barty Eastburn has is a revamped version of a V-8. He's going to look like an idiot."

"No, he's not. Dominic, he has your plans. The real plans for the Vallerio Incorporated engine. The one that Emile worked so hard to design."

Dominic sank into the leather chair next to the desk. How the hell had this happened? "That's not possible. We kept the plans under lock and key. No one knows about the new plans except me and Emile Vallerio. That's it."

"One other person knows, Dominic."

"Angelina?"

"Yes, she has access to your office, *and* you've been living with her for the last six months. I consider her a prime suspect."

"Dammit. That's impossible."

"I'm sorry to be the bearer of bad news, but I called Emile's office, and he said you have the only copy of the plans. I've got enough evidence to go the local authorities. But all they will do is set an injunction against ESP Motors. Do you want me to do that?" Ian asked.

"Who did you talk to in Emile's office? Emile himself?"

"No, he was in a meeting. His assistant, Belle,

answered my questions, and then Emile called me back."

"Go to the authorities, then. Do you have evidence against Angelina?" he asked. He couldn't imagine that she'd betray him again. For one thing, he just didn't believe she could have faked being in love with him.

"Yes. The tape clearly says that De Luca is bringing the plans on the Eurostar from Paris. I met the train in St. Pancras station and Renni was on it."

"Renni's not Angelina. Are you sure she gave him the information?"

"Not a hundred percent, but he works in your factory…do you think he got it himself?"

"I have no idea. Let me talk to Angelina and I'll call you back."

What if she had betrayed him again? What if she were playing him for a fool? But he knew she wasn't. He'd had her watched. Had been careful not to leave any proprietary information in his own office. How would Renni have known where to go?

Deep inside where he'd always feared that he was like Lorenzo Moretti, he was afraid he had the confirmation he'd been looking for. His love for Angelina had brought the Moretti curse down on him.

His love had made him weak, and if not for Ian would have cost Moretti a fortune.

"Dominic?"

"Angelina, come in please. We have a lot to discuss."

"Yes, we do. I believe you were going to tell me," she said.

"Before we get to that," he said, "I need to talk to you about something very important."

"Okay," she said, moving slowly into the room.

She looked uneasy and he knew his attitude wasn't helping. But if there was a leak and it involved her brother, then that meant Renni was in trouble again. That her brother was back to making the same stupid mistakes he had in the past. And this time Angelina wasn't going to be able to bail him out, because he wasn't about to let her sacrifice herself and their happiness for Renni's.

Yet a part of him believed that she might not want to be with him if he put her brother in jail. But he couldn't continue to let De Luca steal from him.

"Are you okay, Dominic? Did Ian give you bad news?" she asked, coming farther into the room.

"I'm fine. Everything is fine. Ian finally got the break he was searching for at ESP Motors."

"Good. Did he find a way to connect Barty to the espionage?" she asked.

"*Sì,* he did. Angelina, I'm not sure how to say this, but the information came from our office."

She blanched. "Do you think I did it?"

He shook his head. How could he have thought that for even a minute? She simply wasn't the type of woman to lie that way. "No, but I think someone close to you did."

He was trying to figure out when Renni could have gone to London to deliver the plans to Barty. Dominic had been in the office for twelve to fourteen hours a day. As he ran over the past week in his mind, he remembered that Renni had driven Angelina to work last week when she'd been too sick to accompany him to the Grand Prix race in Monza in Italy.

"Does ESP Motors have more information from us?"

"They have the new Vallerio engine design."

"How did they get it? I thought Emile kept them," she said.

He had lied to her and everyone else, making sure that the plans were safe in his office. "I had the only copy locked up in my office. Though I know that Emile and his assistant knew this, I don't think the Vallerios would sell us out now."

"No, they wouldn't," she said. She crossed her arms over her stomach, and he'd come to know her well enough to realize she was upset. Really upset. He wondered if her mind had gone along the same path as his to Renni.

"Has your brother had any access to your office?" Dominic asked.

"I didn't let him into your office, Dominic," she said. "Do you think I'd do that? I didn't take those plans and give them to Barty Eastburn. I didn't even know you had them in the office."

"I know that."

"Then how would Renni know?" she asked.

Dominic closed his eyes and reran every encounter he'd had with Renni De Luca. He remembered catching him in the production facility with a woman—a woman who was French. He wondered if she worked for Emile. It made sense.

"What was the name of the woman Renni was with at our reception?"

"Um…I can't remember. Beatrix or Brigitte? Something with a *B*."

"Belle," Dominic said, realizing he'd just found

the answer to how Renni had known that the plans were in his office.

"Yes, that's it. Why?"

"I think I know how your brother knew where to find the plans."

"I…what are you going to do?" she asked.

"What I should have done the first time," Dominic said, getting to his feet. "Put him in jail."

Eleven

Angelina had to get away before she broke down crying. And she wasn't going to get out of Dominic's villa before that happened. She turned to leave, but he stopped her with a hard grip on her arm.

"Where do you think you are going?"

"To ask Gennaro to call me a cab. I can't stay here while you plan to arrest my brother. He's going to need a lawyer and my help. I don't want to listen to any more of your accusations."

"I can't let this go," Dominic said.

She saw the anguish in his eyes, and that did make her cry. "I know."

His mobile rang before she could say anything else and he answered it.

"Moretti here," he said. "Send the cops to arrest Renni. We need to call Emile. He has a leak in his office."

She listened while he talked to Antonio catching him up on everything that had happened. As he talked she tried to piece everything together. How had Renni gotten plans that were only in Dominic's office?

She leaned back against the wall, wrapping her arms around her waist. She was so tired. She really was. The men in her life wore her out.

Damn, Renni. How had he taken the plans and given them to Eastburn? The night of the reception he'd been in an unauthorized area, so she knew he would have no problems getting into any part of the Moretti Motors building. In fact, he'd visited her office a number of times…and when she'd come back from lunch the other day, her keys had been in the in-box.

Had that been it? She needed to find Renni and talk to him. If he'd taken her keys and broken in to Dominic's files, she was never going to forgive him.

Dominic had turned his back on her and she

knew that staying here wasn't going to help anything.

She walked out of the library as quietly and as quickly as she could.

She dialed Renni's number. "Hiya, Ang," he said, answering on the first ring.

"Where are you, Renni?"

"Back in London. I really missed my old life," he said.

"Angelina?" Dominic asked, coming into the hall.

"Gotta go, Ang," Renni said, hanging up.

"Who was that?" Dominic asked.

She shook her head. She couldn't do this. She was trapped between her brother and the man she loved.

"Renaldo?" he guessed.

"Yes."

"Where is he?"

She shook her head again.

"I'm sending you back to Milan," Dominic said. "After this is resolved, I'll call you."

She nodded stiffly. There was no way she could deny him, but would her love change if he had her brother arrested?

Dominic stayed with her until the cab came.

As the cab drove away, she rooted around in her purse for a tissue and blew her nose. Then she took out her mobile phone.

The plans for the new engine had just been finalized and she guessed that Renni would have taken them with him to London. She would have to book herself a flight, but she *was* going there and she *was* going to confront her brother and Eastburn.

She needed to confront her brother and this time prove her loyalty to Dominic.

It had taken Dominic until the time he'd reached Milan to realize that Angelina wasn't the sort of person who would leave confronting her brother to him.

He knew why he'd jumped to conclusions, blamed his own fears of not believing she could really love him and that they could have it all.

He had expected to be betrayed by love, and in a way it had betrayed him and more than likely cost him the only woman he'd ever loved.

He finally realized that she must have gone to London in the hope of confronting Barty. He called his private pilot and had him ready the corporate jet.

He dialed her mobile number, but she still wasn't answering his calls. He called Ian instead.

"This is Stark."

"Ian, I think Angelina is on her way to London. Where are you?"

"I am tailing Eastburn, and he just entered Renaldo De Luca's London flat."

"I'm on my way to London. I don't know where Angelina is, but if she shows up, keep her away from her brother and Eastburn. I don't want her getting hurt," he said.

At least not any more than he had hurt her already. The flight wasn't a long one, but it felt like forever. Dominic tried to work but in the end realized that without Angelina his life would be nothing—his successes were hollow. Now he realized the truth about the Moretti curse.

The truth was that his grandfather and even his brothers to some extent had all cursed themselves. They'd believed they couldn't have love and success, and so had sabotaged their own relationships so that they never had a chance at having it all.

He realized, too, that he'd never told Angelina he loved her, and he regretted that.

As soon as his plane landed he was in the car

he'd had waiting and was speeding across London. Well, that wasn't accurate. The traffic was horrific and he had to stop to buy a congestion ticket to get through London proper to Renni's flat.

When he arrived he found Ian waiting outside with two policemen. "We have a warrant for the arrest of Barty Eastburn and Renaldo De Luca."

"Good. Let's go inside and get them," Dominic said.

"Have you seen Angelina?"

"No, but I had to leave to get the warrant. Let me ask Steve," Ian said, going to check with one of his men. He returned a minute later. "She might be inside. A woman matching her description entered a few minutes ago."

"Dammit," Dominic said.

He realized he didn't care about arresting Barty or Renaldo. He just wanted to find Angelina and hold her in his arms again. He wanted to tell her he loved her and beg her to forgive him for believing she'd betray him.

They climbed the stairs and knocked on Renaldo's door. They heard voices arguing and then the door opened. Barty stood off to one side with a bloody nose and Renni was seated on the couch. Angelina was standing in front of the open door.

The police rushed in and arrested both men. Neither of them said anything as they were cuffed and led away. Ian followed them through the door.

"What about me?" Angelina asked.

"I'm not having you arrested," Dominic said.

"Why not? I thought you believed I was in on it, too."

He shook his head. "Deep inside I didn't believe it."

"Don't do this to me again, Dominic. I love you and that makes it too easy for me to believe the things you say. But now I know you can never trust me."

Dominic drew her into his arms. "I trust you, Angelina. It's myself I've never been able to trust. I've always been afraid that if I loved a woman I'd lose myself, and that was the one thing I didn't want to do."

"Are you saying you love me?" she asked.

"I do love you. More than I ever thought I could love any woman."

"Are you sure?"

"Yes, I am."

"How did you know to come here?" she asked.

"Did you have proof of my innocence before you came to London?"

"No. When you took my car and left Lake Como I realized that you were hurt and angry and then I started to calm down. Once I did I realized you'd never betray me again."

"Because I was afraid of you?" she asked.

"Because you loved me and you aren't the type of woman who would ever betray someone she loves."

"You're right about that," she said.

He kissed her and held her close to him. "I love you, Angelina."

"I love you, too, Dominic."

Dominic didn't let go of Angelina for the rest of the day even when they went to the police station to talk to her brother. Renni hadn't taken the plans out of spite, but to set up Barty so that the other man would leave both of the De Luca siblings alone.

After they got everything straightened out, Angelina and Dominic checked into the Ritz-Carlton and he made love to her in their suite. Only then did the panic in his soul cease. He held her in his arms and looked down at her face. "I do love you."

"I know you do."

"You're going to marry me and give me lots of sons."

"Am I?"

"Will you?" he asked.

"Yes," she said. "Yes, I will."

The next few weeks were long for Angelina and Dominic, but they stood together by Renni's side as he gave compelling evidence against Barty Eastburn. The prosecuting attorney was willing to let Renni off with a reduced sentence of 180 days in jail.

Dominic offered to try to get him off without any jail time, but Renni said that he wanted to take care of this problem on his own. He was tired of having other people rescue him.

"I'm impressed with your brother," Dominic said as they were on his corporate jet heading back to Milan from London.

"Impressed?"

"That he took responsibility for his action. And that he did it for you."

"I know. He wanted to prove to me that he could take care of his own problems."

"Now that your brother is taken care of, you are free of obligations," he said.

"Yes, I am. Why?"

"I have a new task for you."

"Really? What is it?"

"Planning your dream wedding."

"I don't have one. I never thought I'd marry."

"Well, you and I are getting married, and I want the day to be perfect for you."

"As long as you are by my side, it will be," she said.

Epilogue

Lake Como sparkled in the midafternoon sun and the wedding guests milled around the grounds enjoying the festive mood that filled the air. Dominic smiled at his bride across the crowded dance floor. She was currently dancing with his father.

"I can't believe you tied the knot," Antonio said.

"Me either. I think we finally broke the Moretti curse. Now we have a real legacy to leave to our children."

"Children?" Marco asked coming up behind

them. Little Enzo smiled up at Dominic from his father's arms. "Are Nathalie and Angelina expecting?"

"Angelina isn't yet, but we do have a month-long honeymoon planned," he said.

"Nathalie isn't either," Antonio said. "Where are you going? You two have been quiet about the location."

"I bought a house for Angelina in the countryside. Just thirty minutes out of Milan, but I think she'll like it. We are going to go there for the month and settle in. See if it's the kind of place that she's always dreamed of living in."

"Will you be happy there?" Antonio asked. "The commute into Moretti Motors will be long and tedious."

Dominic shrugged. He didn't mind the drive as long as Angelina was happy. She was his life now, not the car company, and with the curse broken he knew they would be happy for the rest of their days. Because he had unraveled the true power of the curse and knew that it had to lie within his own soul.

"You are staring at your bride like a lovesick fool," Marco said.

"I learned the look from you," he said.

"I happen to look very sexy when I stare at my wife," Marco replied.

"Who told you that?" Antonio asked.

"She did," Marco said.

The band switched to an old Nat King Cole song, "Stardust," and Angelina walked toward him. Dominic met her halfway. He pulled her into his arms and danced with her.

"I love you," he said, needing to tell her as often as he could. She'd made his life so complete.

"I love you, too," she said, rising on her tiptoes to kiss him. He kissed her back and then hugged her close. Over her head she saw his parents dancing, their love shining as it always had. And Dominic realized he wanted that for Angelina and himself. Some day, twenty years or so from now, he wanted to dance with her at their child's wedding and still feel as in love with her as he did today.

"What are you thinking?" she asked.

"That you broke the Moretti curse."

"I'm glad I did. I can't imagine life without you."

* * * * *

In honor of our 60th anniversary,
Harlequin® American Romance® is
celebrating by featuring an all-American
male each month, all year long with
MEN MADE IN AMERICA!
This June, we'll be featuring American men
living in the West.

Here's a sneak preview of
THE CHIEF RANGER by Rebecca Winters.

Chief Ranger Vance Rossiter has to confront
the sister of a man who died while under
Vance's watch...and also confront his
attraction to her.

"Chief Ranger Rossiter?" The sight of the woman who'd stepped inside Vance's office brought him to his feet. "I'm Rachel Darrow. Your secretary said I should come right in."

"Please," he said, walking around his desk to shake her hand. At a glance he estimated she was in her midtwenties. Her feminine curves did wonders for the pale blue T-shirt and jeans she was wearing. "Ranger Jarvis informed me there's a young boy with you."

The unfriendly expression in her beautiful green eyes caught him off guard. "Yes," was her clipped reply. "When we arrived in Yosemite the ranger told me I couldn't go anywhere in the park until I talked to you first."

"That's right."

"Knowing you wanted this meeting to be private, he offered to show my nephew around Headquarters."

So this woman was the victim's sister.... "What's his name?"

"Nicky."

The boy who haunted Vance's dreams now had a name. "How old is he?"

"He turned six three weeks ago. Were you the man in charge when my brother and sister-in-law were killed?"

"Yes. To tell you I'm sorry for what happened couldn't begin to convey my feelings."

The woman's gaze didn't flicker. "I won't even try to describe mine. Just tell me one thing. Was their accident preventable?"

"Yes," he answered without hesitation.

"In other words, the people working under you fell asleep on your watch and two lives were snuffed out as a result."

Hearing it put like that, he had to set the record straight. "My staff had nothing to do with it. I, myself, could have prevented the loss of life."

Ms. Darrow's expression hardened. "So you admit culpability."

"Yes. I take full blame."

A look of pain crossed over her features. "You can just stand there and admit it?" Her cry echoed that of his own tortured soul.

"Yes." He sucked in his breath.

"I work for a cruise line. Aboard ship, it's the captain's responsibility to maintain rigid safety regulations. If a disaster like that had happened while he was in charge he would have been relieved of his command and never given another ship again."

Rachel Darrow couldn't know she was preaching to the converted. "If you've come to the park with the intention of bringing a lawsuit against me for negligence, maybe you should." It would only be what he deserved.

"Maybe I will."

In the next instant, she wheeled around and hurried out of his office. Vance could have gone after her, but it would cause a scene, something he was loath to do for a variety of reasons. In the first place, he needed to cool down before he approached her again.

The discovery of the Darrows' frozen bodies had affected every ranger in the park. A little boy had been orphaned—a boy whose aunt was all he had left.

* * * * *

Will Rachel allow Vance to explain—
and will she let him into her heart?
Find out in
THE CHIEF RANGER
Available June 2009 from
Harlequin® American Romance®.

COMING NEXT MONTH

Available June 9, 2009

#1945 THE BRIDE HUNTER—Ann Major
Man of the Month
When he finally locates his runaway bride, he discovers she's been keeping more than a few secrets from him…like the fact th
he's a father!

#1946 SEDUCED INTO A PAPER MARRIAGE—Maureen Child
The Hudsons of Beverly Hills
No one has ever crossed him—until his wife of convenience wal
out on him. Determined to present a united front at the Oscars, h
sets out to reclaim his wife…and their marriage bed.

#1947 WYOMING WEDDING—Sara Orwig
Stetsons & CEOs
His first love has always been money, so when this billionaire marries to get ahead in business, he's completely unprepared for the sparks that fly!

#1948 THE PRODIGAL PRINCE'S SEDUCTION—Olivia Gates
The Castaldini Crown
The prince has no idea his new lover has come to him with ulterior motives. But when he proposes marriage, will he discove
what she's really after?

#1949 VALENTE'S BABY—Maxine Sullivan
Billionaires and Babies
A one-night stand results in a tiny Valente heir. Can this playboy commit to more than just giving his baby his name?

#1950 BEDDED BY BLACKMAIL—Robyn Grady
His suddenly gorgeous housekeeper is about to move on—until
discovers the sizzling passion they share under the covers. Now he'll stop at nothing to keep her there.

SDCNMBPA0